ADVENT

Also by Jane Fraser

The South Westerlies

ADVENT

by

Jane Fraser

HONNO MODERN FICTION

First published in Great Britain in 2021 by Honno Press
'Ailsa Craig', Heol y Cawl, Dinas Powys, Vale of Glamorgan,
Wales, CF64 4AH

1 2 3 4 5 6 7 8 9 10

Published with the financial support of the Books Council of Wales.

ISBN 978-1-912905-25-6 (paperback)
ISBN 978-1-912905-26-3 (ebook)
Cover photograph © Arcangel.com
Cover design: Kari Brownlie
Text design: Elaine Sharples
Printed in Great Britain by CPI Group (UK) Ltd, Croydon CR0 4YY

This novel is dedicated to my parents,
Eleanor and Edward Froom.

Chapter 1

As the train approaches Gowerton North, Ellen reaches for the Gladstone bag she's placed in the overhead luggage net at Liverpool. A gentleman rises from the bench seat opposite and offers to help.

"I can manage, thanks," she says, and then lets out a sigh almost as heavy as the baggage she's carted unaided all the way across the Atlantic. And to think she thought she was travelling light.

She slides open the glass door of the compartment and stands outside in the narrow corridor to look out as the station gets ever nearer, attempting to free the window of condensation with the arm of her coat. Even though it's December, the green shocks: trees, hedges, fields, everything so clean looking and newly washed. She's forgotten how many shades of green there are in Gower. And then remembers the rain.

She's increasingly impatient and taps her sturdy lace-up shoes on the floor. She'll save time standing in the corridor, bag at her side, ready to alight. Doesn't want to waste any more. Been long enough already. Doesn't want to keep the boys waiting either. God knows how long they'll have been at the station, what with the stops and starts she's had to put up with all day, winding her way through the heart of Wales.

She removes the glove from her left hand and stretches out her hand through the small gap in the sliding window that has been left open for ventilation. Feels the moving air. Tests the temperature. It's not cold; more dank and dismal. Yet, despite the mild weather, she's cold: exhaustion, probably. And the smoke that is seeping in is getting to the back of her throat. It's made her filthy. She blows her nose into her handkerchief with gusto – loud and functional – then studies the black smut on the white cotton. Disgusting, yet at the same time, compelling.

She lets herself be lulled by the rhythm of the train, the monotonous chug of the engine, the pattern of the wheels on the tracks. And then the shift from fast to slower and slow as the end of the line approaches.

She knows she doesn't look her best: her face is puffy with the gruelling journey, her complexion, sallow, even wan. She can feel the colour draining out of her. In this mess, she's going to appear older than her twenty-one years. And her hair needs a wash. Even though it's pinned in a tight bun and tucked under her black hat, she can feel her scalp itching. Not at all how she wants to look for a homecoming. She'd wanted to show them. Yes, that's the word: *show* them. Show them how she's changed in two years, show them the woman she's become, the woman who manages alone in a city that everybody goes to, quite unlike this place that everybody comes from.

Everything feels tight and she knows it's not just down to the stays that are digging into her ribcage and abdomen. She'll be glad to finally get home and get them off, kick off her shoes and stockings, change her drawers, shake her hair loose. She wonders whether it will still feel like home when she gets there or whether home is somewhere else these days. No doubt her gut will give her the answer. Or time. She also wonders if on a Thursday there'll be any chance of a bath; any hot water in the copper. It's going to be no holiday. But she had to come.

She recognised in an instant her brother George's fine hand on the envelope: the carefully formed letters, the even, forward slope, the fine loops and swirls. Not a blot of ink anywhere. *Miss. Ellen Thomas. 167, River Avenue, Hoboken, NJ, America.* And when she stood in the scullery where she was cooking lunch for Mrs. Randall, and took the knife and sliced through the edge of the envelope, the contents had ripped at her insides:

He can't last much longer. You know how he is – and there's nothing we can do here to stop him. Perhaps you can talk some sense into him, sis...

All that seems so long ago now, even though it is just short of a month since Mrs. Randall said that she simply must return to Wales for one last Christmas with her ailing father. She'd want her children to do the same for her if they had to. She'd kindly given her the money for the return trip, even if it was the stench of steerage that would have to be endured again.

Your job will be here when you come back, Ellen. If indeed you do come back, she'd said.

So now she's chugging into the little wooden station in this little country from which she set off with just ten pounds in her purse, her Gladstone bag and a forwarding address courtesy of her sponsor, Edward Dix, who had left Llanrhidian earlier. Her *baby* brothers – twins George and Jack – had seen her off, waved her goodbye. They'd been just fifteen then. *Double trouble.* And now they're coming to pick her up again.

She feels the damp chill of coming winter about her, seeping into the peep of ankle between her long dark coat and laced shoes. Two years can feel like a long time, yet like no time at all.

Chapter 2

They're at the end of the platform near the ticket office as the train pulls in, their eyes scouring the emptying carriages for her.

"George! Jack!" she shouts as she charges out of the carriage and through the steam, as they come hurtling towards her.

Jack picks her up and swings her around, kisses her on the cheek and places her carefully back down on the platform. George takes his turn after his brother. All three of them stand still in a tight huddle for a moment in the hiss of the steam, just looking at each other.

"Well, just look at you two," says Ellen, "been standing in manure?"

They smile widely, proud of their obvious maturity, puffing out their chests. Jack takes Ellen's bag as they walk beside the length of the train to the buffers.

"Look well, Nell," says Jack. "Blooming."

"Fibber. Not exactly at my best after six days at sea and a journey all the way from Liverpool in *that*," says Ellen pointing to the engine.

She takes her handkerchief – tucked under her cuff – and blows her nose again as violently as she can.

"Sorry," she says, "but needs must."

"Not very ladylike," says George.

"Well, you know me," says Ellen.

"Must be worn out," says Jack. "Get you back in no time now. They're all ready and waiting for you there."

Ellen strides away, the ground swaying beneath her. The two boys slow to keep pace with her as they leave the cover of the small station and walk towards the pony and trap tethered to the rail in the yard outside. Ellen feels comforted by her younger brothers, the mere, and yet sheer, physical presence of them settling her. At least for the time being.

"Aah, old Celt still going strong, then?" says Ellen as she pats the old grey shire on the nose and leans her own head forward, burrowing deep into his mane.

"Aye, at least *he* is still going strong," says George.

Ellen looks at him, not too tired to read the underlying message. She says nothing. Not yet.

"Smells like home," she says, raising her face from Celt's poll.

At three o'clock in mid-December it is still officially light, but it is drizzling: that monotonous fine, silent drizzle that seems to soak the Gower peninsula from the inside out. Ellen turns her face to feel the rain on her cheek.

"Soft," she whispers. "Not like this in America."

"Aye," says George, "seems like it hasn't stopped since you've been gone. Ground can't take much more. Mild, mind. Too mild. From the south west still."

"Still the old weather-forecaster, then, George? Sound like an old man."

"Still the old sarcastic tone, then, Nell?"

"Don't start now, you two. C'mon we'll have you home within the hour if we can get this old bugger to get a move on," says Jack as he puts Ellen's bag in the back of the trap.

The three of them seat themselves on the bench up front, Ellen in the middle, cushioned between the twins' firm bodies. She turns to each of them, one after the other, pressing her nose in the cloth of their woven coats.

"Lovely," she says. "Can't beat it. Sweat and wool. Like a couple of old rams."

The boys laugh as Jack takes hold of the reins and they pick up a trot along the road that snakes through the marshlands alongside the estuary to the north. George spreads a carthen over Ellen's legs.

"You're exhausted," he says, "feel the damp when you're tired."

She pats his thigh and places her head on his shoulder.

"Does it ever stop raining, here?" she asks, holding her palms up to the sky.

"Only a bit of drizzle," Jack says. "Better than it was. Haven't gone all soft over there, have you?"

Ellen wonders for a moment if she has become hardened, made frostier by the bitter winters. She lets the fine, salty rain soak her cheeks, dampen the strands of hair that have come loose from her bun and are straggling across her face under her black hat. She recalls her grandmother Elizabeth's words: *You'll be all right once you get used to the water over there.* And she'd been right. Once her stomach had settled and her bowels calmed to the hard water of the eastern seaboard, she'd bedded in. But she'd never been able to get her hair to behave there: she missed the gentle Welsh water on her scalp, the silky feel of her long locks after a good egg and vinegar shampoo had been rinsed out.

The rhythm of the trot is soothing and the boys know better than to chunter on when Ellen is tired. By now she is in a trance-like state that only travel and exhaustion can inflict on a body. She gazes out to the estuary on her right as they round the bend into the village of Penclawdd. The signal slows them to a stop as the station master swings closed the gates across the road to let through the train laden with trucks of anthracite. As they wait, Ellen breathes in the air: the salt off the incoming tide is strong, the distinctive stench of shellfish thickening the air. The marsh ponies stand, fetlock high, on mounds of higher ground tufted with reeds, spiking above the River Loughor, which is swollen in the advancing tide. They face shoreward with a surety that they'll be all right: the tide will come in, the tide will go out (just as it always had, just as it always would), and they would get back to roaming and grazing freely until the tide came in again. Ellen feels as though they've been standing there stoically, in that same position, since she said her goodbyes. Here, in Gower, some things never change, but her stomach churns at the thought of what she will find when she gets home to the farm.

As they approach Llanrhidian, she feels her stays constricting her even more, feels one of her headaches coming on. She'll be glad to get in. But then again, she won't.

"Well, what am I to expect, then?" she asks.

"Like I said in the letter. Shadow of the man he was," says George. "Mother's still going hell for leather. Know what she's like. Not much pity for him, mind you."

"Nothing changed, then?" asks Ellen.

"You could say that. Anyway, glad you've come. Mother'll be too, though she probably won't let on. And Gran. Sad to see your son like that, going down the drain. Still the same old Gran. Still sitting in her settle. Never stops talking about you, mind, wondering about her little Nell."

Ellen pulls the carthen tightly around her, feeling an overwhelming sensation of transition and time passing.

As they slow to begin the descent down the steep track into the village of Llanrhidian, Ellen asks Jack to pull up.

"You go on boys," she says, "I'll be with you in a minute. Want to have a bit of a breather."

She needs to feel the ground again, anchor herself through her feet. She has to get her bearings. Prepare herself. She turns to face the estuary, the shore opposite around Llanelli dotted with chimney stacks and plumes of smoke, listless. Beyond that, the mountains of Carmarthenshire and Pembrokeshire, and beyond that, a land across an ocean she can no longer see, a land that was her home.

She turns back to orientate herself. It is only a step now to the farm at Mount Pleasant, the stone house with the thick walls, set under the limestone hill with its commanding location above the village. "A privileged position", her mother used to say with pride, though Ellen had always found the name ironic. As she trudges up the short but steep incline towards her old home, she wonders what has changed there. She recalls her mother: just bits of her and not her face. Mostly that rounded jelly-tussock of a belly which, though her breeding days were long gone, still had a use as a bread board.

She can see her in her place at the side of the kitchen table. In her left hand, she's cradling the newly baked loaf, snuggling the base into the ready stomach-shelf: in her right, she's gripping the large serrated bread knife that she will thrust through the crust and forge through the white dough with a vigorous see-saw motion. She will say grace then and remain on hand, serving the men already seated. And then there are her flat-tipped hands, weathered, veins standing proud. Hands, that had nursed five children and smoothed the hair of the one who'd died. Hands that could tug the udders of cows in the milking shed and pull lambs from ewes in the fields beyond. That could drown kittens in a galvanised bucket – out of sight – and give her brood the occasional slap. And when daylight died, by the light of the paraffin lamp, those same hands would rag Ellen's hair and magic springy ringlets overnight. No doubt her mother will still be sitting in her stick-chair near the range, darning, mending, making do, casting on the wool she spun and clickety-clacking her way through the hours; knit-one-purl-one, ribbing the patterns embedded in her head.

*

As she approaches, the sight of his familiar working boots abandoned outside the kitchen door signals that her father, William, is in. That he hasn't gone for a drink yet. From generation to generation, those boots just waiting to be stepped into.

There they all are in the kitchen as she envisaged, in their allocated positions: her mother Eleanor, her father, and her grandmother, Elizabeth. She wonders whether they stirred at all in the intervening years. But now as she enters they rouse themselves – those that can – standing up and inching forward, waiting their turn to welcome her. William remains seated in his place at the right of the range, in his familiar horsehair chair, with the winged backrest, the stuffing worming out of the faded upholstery. Ellen feels herself draining at the sight of his face which tells its own story: so empty, so broken. Time has caught up with him. She loses focus, and before her eyes appear colourless zigzag patterns followed by numbness and nausea: all tell-tale signs of a bad headache. She swallows hard before speaking:

"Father. Good to see you. Missed you so much," she says.

He still doesn't rise from the chair so she bends to plant a kiss on his brow, just as she'd always done. But now her lips feel the clamminess of his sallow, almost tallow skin. The sweet-stale smell of alcohol on his breath is as familiar as the kiss; but she says nothing about that as his eyes fill up.

She is aware of her mother's needy stare, looking on at the scene from her place at the other side of the range; waiting her turn to greet her. Scenes she looked over all her life. Her face, like the range, has lost its shine: her white hair is even whiter, her hands fiddle with her apron. Ellen walks towards her, arms outstretched. She notices her mother's eyes welling with tears. This is a first.

Never before has Ellen seen her mother even on the verge of crying. She hands her mother the handkerchief from up her sleeve to dab her eyes, and through the tears, the three women smile at the filth smeared on it.

"No thanks," says Eleanor and wipes her face with her pinny instead.

"It's lovely to see you. Mother. Good to be home. How are you coping?" she asks as she stoops to kiss her.

"As well as can be expected, considering," she replies in a low tone, placing the emphasis on *considering* and throwing at William one of the looks that Ellen well remembers, while he remains seemingly oblivious in the chair. Eleanor turns her cheek to accept Ellen's kiss and raises her chin and her shoulders in an unusual harmony, as if trying to keep herself from being engulfed by rising water. Beyond Eleanor is Elizabeth, her grandmother, hunched over with a stick, at one end of her favourite settle in the corner where she has sat forever, trying to keep the draught off her.

"My darling Nell, welcome home, we've mizzed thee, maid – much too much, if truth be told," says Elizabeth in that old Gower way of hers. Her grandmother's voice is like a lullaby and when Elizabeth embraces her, it feels of days past; the warmth of the range in winter and hot, buttered toast done on the toasting fork.

"Come and sit down at the table, here, Ellen," says Eleanor, "nice cup of tea and a bit of cake. You must be whacked."

George pulls out a chair for her. It scrapes across the quarry tiles. It has only been a couple of minutes, but Ellen feels as though she has never been away. The light is fading fast from the kitchen with its two small windows, one back, one front, the ceilings low and beamed. Same smells: hams hanging from the charnel, damp washing draped over the kitchen maid above the range, whitepot baking in the oven. Ellen's mood descends with the dusk, and there's a growing tightness in her diaphragm which is not just the stays holding her in place.

"Make yourself useful, Jack," says Ellen, "let's get a bit of light in here. I'm all out of kilter."

Jack lights the paraffin lamp and brings it to the centre of the scrubbed pine table.

"Let there be light. And behold there was light," he jokes.

"No need for that, Jack," says Eleanor. "Just do as she says. Earn your keep."

George pulls up his chair to the table.

"Will you be joining us, Mother?" Eleanor asks Elizabeth who is cwtching up in the settle.

"I'll have mine in the hand, on my lap, if that's all right with you, dear?" she says.

"And William. What about you? Or need I ask?"

William raises his right hand and Ellen watches her mother respond to the signal which Eleanor has long learned to interpret: *don't bother me with trifles, leave me alone I'm all right just where I am, thank you.*

13

"I'll bring you a cup over, then," she says, muttering under her breath as she walks to the range.

Ellen looks on as Eleanor begins her tasks on cue just as she predicted. She stands at the side of the range while the copper comes to the boil, measuring out one scoop of tea from the caddy for everyone present and then adding 'one for the pot' just as she's always done. She pours the boiling water, puts the lid on and then dresses the pot in one of her knitted tea cosies.

"Just let it steep for a couple of minutes," she instructs as she brings it over to the table.

She carries the whitepot to the table, too, and cuts a small slice for everyone. The aroma of currants and sugar fills the air. Ellen notices that her mother has got the best china cups and saucers and tea plates off the dresser, as though expecting royalty. The smooth porcelain with the delicate rosebud patterns seems out of place next to the hands of her twin brothers folded on the table top. And her own, if she's honest. She knows she is hardly a prize English – or Welsh – rose. Her hands show she hasn't been afraid of hard work in her twenty-one years, and her arms could give her brothers' a run for their money. She'd have made a good farmer's wife, she thinks. No, she'd have made a good farmer. Eleanor pours for everyone, trapping the loose tea in the strainer and then discarding the slops into a small basin. She sees to Elizabeth with her tea and a bit of cake in the saucer, takes over a cup for William, places it on the arm of the chair and shouts, 'Mind you don't spill.' Ellen wonders if her father is now hard of hearing as well as everything else that's befalling him, or if

14

her mother's words are falling on deliberately deaf ears. She can't blame him, really.

With everyone sorted as best as she can, Eleanor finally joins all of them around the table. Ellen recalls the days when there had been so many of them arranged around it, the surface now etched with the scratches and grooves of time. She remembers the first George and the accident, and her big sister, Hannah, three years older than her, married to some publican named Charlie Redding, much to her mother's disgust. And then there is Ellen herself, sitting again in the same chair, in the same place as she'd always done back then. Its worn, warm timbers seem to accommodate her behind perfectly. The twins sit on opposite sides of the table, nearest the door to the yard. Ellen watches as they both pour their tea into their saucers, hunch over and slurp the liquid without saying a word. Until then Ellen forgot how everyone in the room takes their tea the same way: weak, no milk, no sugar, the Gower way.

Chapter 3

Men can't hang about all evening in the kitchen, doing nothing, Jack says. Much as it is lovely to have Ellen home, there is work to be done. Men's work. It can't wait. He and George will leave them to it while they go outside to do what needs doing. The stock that is undercover in the stalls in the yard needs checking and seeing to; hay, feed and the like. Celt, poor old dab, has to be stabled up, the cart put away in the sheds.

"I'm off," says the old man William, getting up from the chair and reaching for his coat from the hooks.

"Tonight? Are you joking? Your daughter's just got home, travelled all this way, and you're off?" shouts Eleanor, her voice cracking with the volume or the strain, Ellen can't tell.

But it falls on deaf ears.

"Leave it, Mother. I'm tired, anyway. We'll talk tomorrow, Father. It's all right," she says as she gets up and helps him on with his coat.

"You're too soft with him, my girl. Always were. Hasn't done him any good. Hell bent on destroying himself, he is. Go you then, William. Be it on your own head."

Eleanor clears away the dishes and sets the table ready for

the morning as she always does, but with more noise than Ellen remembers. Ellen tries to make her sit down, but she stays on her feet.

"Like to stay ahead of myself," Eleanor says, "keep on top of things. But you stay there, you, I can manage."

Tonight Ellen will not argue with that. Perhaps her mother does for once acknowledge that she is tired, she has nothing more to give, has only the capacity to sit and let others take the helm. She wonders if her mother has any idea of just how far she has travelled and under what conditions. Her mother who has never in her whole fifty-five years been east of Swansea.

Even though she is beyond exhaustion, she feels the need to be clean before she takes to her bed, like the finickity ritual of the one farm cat that is allowed inside, licking its fur from ear to tail before it can lie coiled in a purring bliss on the mat in front of the range.

"Any chance of a bath?" asks Ellen. "Know it's Thursday, but I'm stinking to high heaven. These clothes are walking. Been on for a week."

"I'll nip and get it," says Eleanor, "plenty of hot water in the copper. You can have a good soak in front of the range."

Ellen thanks her mother and watches her disappear out of the kitchen door.

She comes back from the dairy adjacent to the kitchen with the galvanised tin bath and a jug.

"Get out the way. Skit, puss," shouts Eleanor at the cat as she kicks it out of the way and sets the bath down in front of the range. Everything is on the boil – kettles, saucepans of every size, pots and pans – and when the steam rises, she pours the hot water into the bath until it is half full.

"There," she says, "not like America, I know. But it'll do. I'll get some towels. Leave it cool down a bit. Don't want you scalding yourself. Enough on my plate."

Ellen stands by the range while her mother holds up a large sheet she's taken from the cupboard, her grandmother on the settle in the corner. She feels little embarrassment tonight as she unclasps the brooch at her neck, unbuttons her long dark dress and raises it over her head, dropping it in a heap on the floor. As the fabric comes into contact with her hair, there is the crackle of static. She puts her palm to her head and feels some strands of her hair, rise and come to meet it.

"Look like a wild one," Eleanor says to her.

"Feel like a wild one," says Ellen.

Ellen discards her chemise next; it is creased and yellow underneath, so it joins the crumpled dress on the tiles.

"That's better," she says with a loud outbreath as she unclasps her stays.

She unhooks her brassiere and stands there on the mat, naked apart from her large, white drawers. Her breasts are heavy and sore. When she takes off her knickers she can see why.

"That's all I need," she says. "Must be all the travelling."

"What?" says Eleanor.

She points to her soiled pants on the floor.

"Oh! I never thought you would..." says Eleanor. "That's a turn up for the books."

"Just after I got to America. Still all over the place, mind."

After Ellen has immersed herself in the bath, her mother drops the sheet and starts bundling up the discarded clothes.

"I'll put these drawers ready for the wash," she says. "Bit of spit, cold water, make a bit of a paste. Let them sit awhile. That should get the blood out."

"A remedy for everything, Mother," says Ellen sarcastically. "If only everything were as easy to blot out, eh?"

Eleanor makes no comment; just sighs, and carries on gathering up the clothes to take to the outhouse to launder next morning.

"A woman, now," shouts Elizabeth from the corner.

"Can breed all I like and be happy then, just like you lot," says Ellen.

"No need to be like that," says Eleanor.

"It's not the be all and end all, you know," says Ellen.

"Well, that's a matter of opinion. I mean, if it hadn't been for *that*, you'd never have gone, would you? Would have changed everything."

"Who knows?" says Ellen.

Why would they think *that* was the only reason? It wasn't the whole story. Can't they see that she is different from them, always has been? That her feet were itching to get away? Choose not to see it, probably, because of what it exposes in them. Don't want to think about how stuck they are. Rooted. Especially Mother. Imprisoned by her womb. By the farm. By the men. By being a woman. Can't bear to think that there are those in this world that are not like her. But, Gran – she's on her side. At least, most of the time. There's a strong will still there in that withered relic in the corner.

But they are half right. She'll give them that much. Her face reddens as she knows *that* was the catalyst to pack her bags and do what she'd been thinking about for longer than they'll ever know. The warmth of the water cannot blot out the past the way her mother will the tell-tale blood on her drawers. All the rejection and humiliation come bubbling up to the surface. But she'd had to be honest, had to tell him that she didn't menstruate. Perhaps she shouldn't have been so honest. Just let time tick by. It might have happened. Then again it might not have. She had to get away from him and this place for good. Gower was not a place for a woman with a broken heart and a useless womb. A woman who couldn't be bred. Richard Tucker. It was easier to forget someone when you were away, when you weren't within touching distance, likely to breathe the same air – or worse: see him with a woman on his arm who *was* fit for purpose.

"Mother, wash my back, please? A real good scrub. Plenty of lather," she instructs.

Eleanor takes the flannel and rubs it with the bar of carbolic soap. She starts at the nape of Ellen's neck, rubbing hard in small, circular motions, working her way down.

"Don't want to get your hair wet. Not at this hour," Eleanor says. "You'll catch your death."

"For goodness sake, Mother. What's this stuff about washing your hair? Don't wash your hair late. Don't wash your hair if you're *unwell*. Don't wash your hair too often or you'll wash all the natural oils out of it. I'm washing my hair. It's filthy. Hand me the jug. Now."

Ellen senses that her mother likes being told what to do for a change. She feels it in the rhythmic rubbing of her mother's hands along her spine, soothing her body and perhaps allowing her mind to hand itself over to the rote, physical action of soap on skin for a brief few moments along with the handover of the jug. Ellen unpins her hair and lets it loose. It falls heavily past her shoulders, almost to her waist, in thick, dark waves that look as though they should never be imprisoned in clips, as though they're longing to come undone. She leans her head back as Eleanor pours the water from the jug over her hair, smoothing her forehead to keep the water out of her eyes just like she did when she was a child.

"Takes some soaking, this lot," says Eleanor. "Water's running black."

"Soot from the train. Disgusting."

"I'll give it a good rub, now," says Eleanor.

"How's the water?" shouts Elizabeth from the corner.

"Beautiful," says Ellen. "Forgotten how soft it was."

She gives herself up again to those hands of her mother's, the fingertips strong – rough even – on her scalp as she soaps her up. Two rinses. The first for cleanliness. The second for shine. Forget about the Godliness.

"There. Now you'll know it's had a good wash," Eleanor says as she brings a towel to wrap around her hair. "Don't let the water get cold, though."

"I'll do as I'm told, Mother," says Ellen, "for tonight."

"It's good to have you home, you know," says Eleanor.

Cleansed and purged, Ellen is soon sitting in front of the range, covered from head to toe in her long flannelette nightgown, the cat keeping her feet warm. Her mother stands behind her, towel-drying her hair, and she brushes it at least one hundred times. She knows that Ellen cannot possibly go to bed with wet or tangled hair, God knows what might become of her if she did.

Later, candle in hand, Ellen walks past the closed door of the parlour on her way to bed. She mounts the steep staircase, remembering every creak on the third, eighth, and final tread. She's forgotten how low the ceiling is along the upstairs landing, and even though she isn't tall, she feels the unnecessary need to stoop: there seemed to be so much more space in Hoboken, the rooms bigger, airier – more oxygen.

She turns the brass door knob to her bedroom at the end of the corridor. It faces north and as she enters, she can see the glimmer of lights across the estuary in Llanelli. They look quite inadequate, she thinks: she's got used to the bright lights at night seen from her room at Mrs. Randall's. Over there, Ellen leaves the curtains open so that she might sleep better. Even the windows sometimes, so that the noise floods in all night long: trams, the odd car, voices. She doesn't seem so alone with the world carrying on outside. Here, in the dark, with her own thoughts, it feels as if everything has been muted, exposing her inner self.

She places the sputtering candle on the bedside table, on top of the white crocheted runners made by her grandmother.

In the flickering light, she looks around the bedroom: everything just as she'd left it. Here is the iron and brass bedstead with the metal frame. She presses the feather mattress with her hands, feels the dip in the middle where she and Hannah had always rolled into the centre. Here is the oak chest of drawers with the brass-ingrained handles, overlarge for the proportions of the small room, looming against the back lime-washed wall. She walks over to it and opens one of the drawers: it slides soundless on runners made with perfect dovetailing. The smell of mothballs hits her in the stomach and sours the room.

Next to the drawers, in the corner, is a small dresser with a blue and white china jug and bowl. Cold winter mornings, a quick swill before getting off to school.

And here also is a single shelf on which are arranged the few books she ever had access to, earned mostly for good attendance at Sunday School. She fingers the spines, takes one down, brings it close to her nose and inhales the smell of old print, the mustiness of the passing years. She places it back in position. It is late.

She pads back to the bed over which hangs the sampler she made in school. Inside the mahogany frame, a large red brick house, three windows upstairs, two down, a porch in the centre, a high-pitched roof with chimneys at either end, a small path, flowers around the edge. It was done in cross-stitch, mostly, with some stem stitch and running stitch. She thinks back to the skeins of silk threads, the crimsons, the creams, the greens; the needles with which she'd deliberately prick the tip of her left index finger to draw blood, squeezing the flesh until it dribbled scarlet as she continued to pull the thread through the tiny hole. There was no pain. All that performance just to relieve the boredom of needlework. She sees her name as artist: Ellen Thomas, aged 10, Llanrhidian Parochial School, 1893. HOME SWEET HOME in bold block capitals staring back at her. She wonders where that girl went.

She pulls up the sheets, enjoys the weight of the carthen and the eiderdown pressing down upon her. Once she shared this intimate space with Hannah: mumps and measles, laughter and tantrums, fears and even dreams. As they got older, there was the tang of overnight urine in the chamber pot under the bed, the sweat from their adolescent bodies and the distinctive metallic smell of Hannah's breath – like iron filings – each month after her sister started her periods. The blood flowed freely while they slept together. But it hadn't flowed for her.

She closes her eyes for a few moments and thinks about how life might have turned out. She could have ended up, in her allocated place, at the side of a kitchen table on a different farm, not that far from here, the whole life being squeezed out of her in a twelve-by-twelve kitchen. She'd have put on the pinny when she married Richard, and gone to his sixth-generation family home. She'd have got him – and his father, Matthias, and brother, Harold, into the bargain, job lot – all the days of her life until his father had gone to join his dead wife and all those other Tuckers now silent and mouldering under their tombstones at St. Illtyd's and St. Rhidian's. There'd have been a child, no doubt; a boy if they were lucky, who'd grow, bring home a wife who'd bring forth a child. Ellen saw it all playing out, the life not lived: the big-bellied wife at the side of the table. Ellen had never really seen herself as a big-bellied woman at the side of a table. Or maybe this was what she thought now because it hadn't worked out the way she planned?

Empty now, she lies restless. Her feelings have been all over the place – up and down all day – and she just wants to find sleep. But old wounds that she wishes would have finally scabbed-over and healed, were picked open by her mother at bath time. She wonders if reading might calm her, that she might find comfort in words she loves.

She rises from the unease of her bed and returns to the books. Her hand comes to rest on the hard cover with its embossed title: *The Pilgrim's Progress*. Back in bed, she flicks through its leaves. But it isn't the words printed on the page that she is drawn to, but the flimsy sheet of paper, folded into four small squares and tucked into the crease of the page. The ink is fading, but the memory is fresh, as though it were written yesterday. She reads the dedication:

To Richard
You are the life and soul of the
land and life I love

Ellen Thomas 25th November 1901

Chapter 4

At the top of the hour, the grandfather clock chimes eleven. Eleanor looks up from her knitting as the reverberation fills the room. She glances towards the clock face, as if to confirm to herself that it really has reached this time.

For the last two hours, she marked the minutes by the heavy swing of the pendulum in the wooden case. She listened to the repetitive ticking of the hands and the monotonous strikes on the hour: on the quarter past, the half, the three-quarters. William is often as late as this, she tells herself. And now, even with his favourite home, she sits waiting. Always waiting.

Whether it's Tuesdays at the Welcome to Town, Wednesdays at the Dolphin Inn, or the rest of the week at the Greyhound Inn or the King's Head, it makes no difference. As far as she is concerned, they are all dens of iniquity. Her stomach curdles as she imagines him and all those men there, knowing full-well that they draw their curtains tight, bolt their doors from the inside, swish the long, blue, velvet drapes across the brass rails to keep out the draught, keep down the noise within, obscure any cracks of light from any stray policemen on the prowl. Locked inside, they sit drinking and gambling and carousing in the smoke-filled, low-ceilinged back-rooms after hours, long after the landlords call time and the bells are rung and the men sit in their private worlds away from their women. They swill ales and grow loud and coarse like pack animals, thinking they're safe from their wives and sweethearts. They are arm-wrestling, man to man, forearm to forearm, sinew to sinew, beer spilling over the rims of their pewter measures, the frothy headed hops slopping onto the copper-topped tables and soaking into the sawdust covered floor. Yes, she can see clearly the upturned decks of cards on the table, the shuffle and the deal, the eyes intent and elusive above the fans of black spades and red diamonds held tightly in gnarled fingers. Can hear the money clink on the metal: the florins, half crowns, crowns and the sovereigns changing hands. And the land. Her land. Sometimes she's sure she can hear the dogs baying and yelping in the pits or in the barns out the back as they rip each other's flesh apart, the squeals of the cocks as they fight to the death among the guffaws and cheers of men over-loud in her burning ears.

There is often the urge to rise from her half-empty bed, where she has lain long, turning the pillow over and over again in search of cool, ruminating on the injustice of it all. She imagines reaching for her coat from the peg and thrusting it on over her long flannel nightgown, leaving it open, her nightdress on show to the world, should it care to see. Her grey hair is loose and flying out behind her in her frenzy as she steps into her boots and races to the sheds where the crooks are lined up against the wall.

Under the light of the full moon, she is running then,

crazed with anger and righteousness, running like a young woman, her legs light and fleet, free of the varicose veins, the fluid on the knee and the swollen ankles. And she keeps on running until she comes to the inn where she knows he'll be with his cronies. And she'll go in, a woman on her own into the inner cell, and they'll all be in there at the bar, at the tables, and they'll turn and look at her as she bares her sagging, redundant breasts, digging her nails deep into her chest till the crinkled skin splits and the blood runs free and the hurting eases.

And then the men will turn and look at William, with perhaps pity or perhaps incomprehension, waiting for his reaction. But she won't care. She'll meet him eye to eye in this hallowed space and keep her gaze fixed and take the crook and hook him around the neck and drag him out as she screams: *Get home you bastard, you selfish bastard. Can't you see what you're doing to yourself, to us?*

But she didn't do it. Not that brave a woman. Rather, she stayed paralysed in the cold bed, her gut churning, her heart palpitating for the man she once loved, the father of her children, waiting for him to come back. And tonight, again, he's still there – wherever he is – gambling their futures away with the drink, pissing it away up against a hedge or vomiting it onto some filthy track as his feet try to find his way home to her.

Say nothing's best, maid, her mother-in-law, Elizabeth, often tells her from her settle in the corner. *No point getting all upset. If he'll listen to anyone, he'll listen to Nell. But I doubt it. Too far gone, now.* The old woman sees her son stagger home, night after night, a wreck of a man, reeking of spirits and often with less acreage than he'd set out with. She feels him shrinking away, shrinking their lives with him; frittering away their foundations and hopes for the future. She feels him slipping through her hands like water. *He'll be the death of me*, she says though she knows he'll be gone before her.

Eleanor and Elizabeth are already mourning for the husband and son that William once was. The love has morphed into a feeling of helplessness that drags them down. The top fields at Welsh Moor gone, the lower rich pastures near Crichton and Llethryd gone, and more recently – the latest indignity, as Eleanor puts it – the Croft: six acres of grass so green at the heart of the village, lost in some never-to-be-mentioned deal. Just six acres, but six acres that spoke of what the Thomases were and what they were becoming. A meagre forty acres is all that remains of Mount Pleasant. *Not enough to keep the cat,* Eleanor spat at William before he went out of the door, *leave alone two slabs of men.*

She snuffs out the lamp and takes herself off to bed, leaving Elizabeth snoring in the corner and her husband to find his own way up the stairs.

Chapter 5

Just after dawn, Eleanor pulls open the curtains of the kitchen windows – back and front – with a flourish to signal that a new day has begun despite the night before. The window at the front of the house looks onto the yard, the lane, the village, the world beyond. The one at the back looks out across the kitchen garden in the lee of the limestone hill. The shock of the transition from dark to light is stark. Now that the mild wet front has passed through, the harsh glare of low winter sunlight slices into the room like a knife with a flint-white flash.

Eleanor stands looking out. William is in his little allotment.

She opens the kitchen door and calls the boys already working out in the yard and yells up to Ellen that breakfast will be ready in a few minutes.

The boys take off their boots as they come into the kitchen.

Ellen yawns and stretches like the cat as she comes down the stairs. "What time did he get in?"

"Don't ask me. Fasto, I was," says Eleanor. "Past caring and not wasting any more sleep. Lost cause. In the devil's grip."

"Don't be so hard on him, Mother. He can't help it."

"Can't help it? His choice. And look. He's up there already with those blessed vegetables."

The boys rise from the table and come to stand one each side of their mother and sister. They look out through the small, south-facing window which backs onto the high stone retaining wall. Directly opposite the kitchen door, there's a flight of well-worn stone steps leading to the allotment at the top.

"Good for the soil, this frost," says Ellen. "Break the clods down a treat. Lovely tilth ready for planting. He'll like that! Always one for his veg."

They watch him there, down on bended knees on the crusted earth.

"Don't know what he finds to do all day up there," says Eleanor. "Each to their own, I suppose."

"It's his life," says Jack. "Keeps him going."

"Mmm," sighs Eleanor "Pity it isn't his family."

But she knows deep inside how William loves the feel of the cold soil on his bare hands. The smell of the rich, damp, Gower earth. How in winter he enjoys the sensation of the sole of his boot coming down on the edge of the snawl, the pressure in breaking through the top crust with the prongs, digging down deep to lift and shake, and lift and shake, the brown-black soil beneath his feet.

Even though the vegetable patch is large, he tends it single-handedly. Lovingly. Through the cold months he grows winter roots in one half, swedes, parsnips, turnips and sets of onions. He lets the other half lie, for the frost to get

31

at it, and then he feeds it with fresh manure from the horses and the vegetable waste from the kitchen that they leave rot down.

She knows he loves it there, the solitude, engrossed in the care of a patch of land that is within his control. He enjoys seeing the fruits of his labour. It satisfies what soul he has left. More so than religion.

He never fails to appreciate the marvel of growth. Enjoys the fact that he can create wonders from seeds he plants when the soil is tilled and raked and sifted and warm and well-watered. When the conditions are right for things to flourish. It takes him away for a while from the thoughts of their boy. The first George. The one they loved and lost. The one *he* lost. The one he can't watch grow.

Through the window, the other George sees his father on the grass at the edge of the earth, rubbing his hands together to free the dirt. Still on his knees, he looks up towards the heavens, raising his hands with both his palms upwards as though asking a question, as though hoping for an answer.

Jack has been hoping too. Hoping that if life had played out differently and his father hadn't hit the bottle, he'd have taken on a sizeable farm when the time came. As the elder son, if only just, it's the way it is. It was never a rich farm in terms of acres and yields, as some were on the peninsula, but it would have been rich enough for him and Annie when he marries her and brings her to live at Mount Pleasant, when the time comes. It might have been rich enough to give George a living too at one time. Perhaps they even could have run it together, a thought that is now impossible.

It was about one hundred and fifty acres when the twins were young, a few acres here, a few acres there, spread out across the parishes of Llanrhidian Higher and Llanrhidian Lower, as was the way in these parts. There were good fields. There were those that were not so good. There was high pasture on the edge of the Bryn and low pasture that abutted the marsh. And thank God there were commoners' rights too so they could supplement their income with access to free roaming rights on Cefn Bryn, put sheep and ponies out to graze on the salt marshes. It was a good mixed farm like most in the area: Gower earlies, because of the mild climate and the south westerly wind, caulis and root vegetables, cattle, sheep, a few pigs, and poultry. They'd got by on this once upon a time. Got by quite nicely.

Jack all of a sudden feels the burden of responsibility, like cloying mud on his work boots, dragging him down. There's going to be a lot to sort out one day.

There comes a loud and rhythmic tapping from the other end of the room. At first they think it's Elizabeth's cane on the floor as some kind of alarm call, but as they turn, they see she's dropped off, chin on chest, mouth open and snoring loosely. The sound is emanating from the window at her side, an incessant rat-a-tat-tatting at the glass. Eleanor can see a dark shape outside the glass, a beak pecking at the panes, the outline of fluted wings, outstretched claws.

"Get it away from here. Quick," she hollers, clapping her hands. "Shoo!"

"What's happening?" mumbles Elizabeth, waking with a start.

"Only an old crow, Gran," says George as he waves his arms the way he does with the sheep.

The crow stands motionless for a second, fixing its jet pupils on Eleanor.

"Never liked a crow," says Eleanor.

"Just superstition," says Jack.

With that the crow takes flight in a frenzy of feathers, as Eleanor tugs the curtains back tight.

Chapter 6

On Christmas Eve, Jack and George hang around the kitchen table like Salt and Pepper, the farm collies. Tongues itching, they salivate, waiting for their mother and sister to finish filling up the white china pudding basins and scrape the earthenware mixing bowls clean. Until they're done, they sit still, not saying a word, already tasting that first lick of the wooden spoon. "Age before beauty," Ellen says as she passes Jack the spoon. There's a warm feeling in her gut on this special day, realising that for once her mother has not stuck to her usual routine of doing the puddings on stir-up Sunday at the beginning of the month but has waited for her to arrive home, to do things as a family. She'd missed all her family on the last two Thanksgivings. But now's not the time to chat about all the things that are different in America.

Jack pokes out his tongue until it aches, to taunt George who he then reminds is his younger brother even if it's by just five minutes. He then says an over-loud *Mmm* as he wipes his lips free of the Christmas pudding mix with the back of his hand.

"Leave some for me," says George. "It's not fair. He always gets everything first."

Their mother grabs the spoon off Jack and tips the bowl at an angle towards her to go in deep for the final scrape.

"There," she says handing the spoon to George. "Don't be such a baby."

"Yes, don't be such a baby," mimics Jack.

Though they're seventeen, on this special day they long to be much younger, to be children again rather than the hard-working men they've had to become. They want to believe in something they don't believe in anymore, like Father Christmas, for things to be like they were once upon a time.

The smells in the kitchen are still the same as past Christmases: the giblets from the goose they plucked earlier in the shed are simmering in a pot on the range, in readiness for tomorrow's gravy, the goose is trussed and stuffed and lies in a roasting tray, and soaked currants, fruit peel and rum sweeten the air. Even Ellen is home. For a few minutes, it is enough to warm their bellies, to make believe.

"Right, you two. Make a wish," says their mother. "Younger man first, this time."

George takes a sixpenny bit from his mother's hand. It's silver and shiny. Newly minted. The head of the King sparkles on the face of it, ushering in a fresh reign, a fresh century. George pokes the tanner into the depths of the pudding mix in one of the basins, closes his eyes, makes his wish. Then Jack does the same in the other.

"What d'you wish for?" asks Jack.

"Can't say. Won't come true if you tell."

They lean across the table resting on their elbows, their

faces on their hands, watching the women cover the basins with white muslin. When they are finished with that, they secure the fine cloth with twine, tie bows, double-knotted.

"Done," Eleanor says. "A good job jobbed. Pity your father isn't around, though; but there you are."

For a second Jack makes eye contact with Ellen then averts his gaze and shifts it across to the empty, winged armchair at the side of the range. Though he has upped and left it earlier, for the pub again, it seems to retain him – arms shabby and worn with age, horsehair stuffing peeping out of the upholstery of the bald seat. Even his odour has impregnated the fabric: the sweet-sour alcohol of his breath, the tang of sweat from his ailing body.

Jack looks back at his mother and notices she's taking off her apron and draping it across the back of her chair. Sometimes he wonders if it's the wrapping of the apron and the criss-crossing of the ties that hold her together, that if she kept it off for too long she would fall to pieces. She brushes down the pleats of her long, drab dress, rearranges the material as if she's expecting someone. She swishes across the quarry tiles to stand in front of the mirror on the wall where she checks her face, wipes away the flour that has further whitened her hair and coated her left cheek. She looks up at the sound of the grandmother clock striking the hour.

"It's very dark for three o'clock," she says walking to the window.

Jack and George join their mother and Ellen at the front

window to see that snow is falling, thick, dense flakes floating past the glass.

"Looks like it might stick," says George.

"Is there anything you can't predict?" asks Ellen, laughing at George's unfailing acumen.

"Not when it comes to the weather. It's cold enough to stick. We're in for it good and proper," he continues, looking out over the estuary.

"Just enjoy the magic for a while," says his mother. "Don't worry so much."

All the way out to the horizon, smudging the boundary between water and sky, the snow clouds hang low and heavy, the colour of the pewter plates on the kitchen dresser. Unusually, there is no wind. Through the window the world looks calm and soft and still just like in the carols.

"D'you think Father'll be all right in this?" asks George, tugging at the neck of his pullover.

"He'll be hunkered down with his old cronies in the back of some inn somewhere Door locked. Curtains drawn. Be oblivious to the snow," his mother says. "Anyway, said he'd be in by five at the latest. Promised. I'm taking down a ham especially. If he's not back by then, we'll send out a search party."

Without needing to be asked, George takes a spill and opens the range door. He carries the flame to light the lamps, which cast a soft glow throughout the room, helping to lift the gloom of late afternoon.

"C'mon boys, let's get in the Christmas spirit," Eleanor says. "Can't wait all day for him. Put our lives on hold."

She walks to the dresser and opens one of the cupboards at the base.

"Here's yours, Jack," she says as she hands him the blue stocking she knitted soon after he was born. It's darned at the heel. Jack takes it from her and presses it to his face. It gives off camphor and oiled wool, like a wet fleece.

"Smells like Christmas," he says as he rushes to the range and searches out the old nail under the mantelshelf that his father had knocked in the underside of the timber. For as long as he can remember this is where he has hung his stocking on Christmas Eve. Always hoping.

"And yours, George. Bit worse for wear, this one. Moths have been at it!" she says.

"Doesn't matter."

And he hangs his grey-holed stocking from the nail at the other side of the shelf.

Tomorrow they might be stuffed with monkey nuts, sweetmeats, a cotton handkerchief; a blacklead, if they are lucky.

"So where's mine, Mother?" asks Ellen.

"Chucked yours," she says. "Didn't think you'd be needing it anymore."

"Well that's nice. Don't worry, I'll hang my own stockings up."

"I've got some holly, too. It's in the pantry, George," says Eleanor. "No berries, though. Not this year. Birds have had them all. Should have known it was going to snow."

The clock ticks on. At the top of the hour, the quarter past, the half past, the quarter to, they all look up as the strikes fill the room. They don't say much to each other, but the words are there in the eyes as time stretches on.

The curtains are left open and from the table the boys take a break from the dominoes and draughts, to keep watch on the snow. It's still falling soundlessly and from the warmth of the kitchen, the scene outside takes on the magic of a fairytale. A white pillow is forming on the window sill. The candle in the recess illuminates the whiteness; but it doesn't draw their father home. Not yet.

The growl of Jack's stomach sounds through the kitchen.

"We'll give him till seven. I know you're all starving, but perhaps he's waiting for the snow to stop. It can't go on like this much longer. Lay the table, Ellen. Clear away, boys," Eleanor commands.

Ellen walks to the dresser and takes out a white damask cloth from the drawer and the best napkins, starched and flat-ironed, folded and pressed into triangles. She takes a corner of the cloth, Eleanor takes the other end and they cast it across the scrubbed table. It billows out like a large cloud before they smooth it out across the surface, hiding the cracks and stains underneath.

Ellen sets the table for six, assuming Gran will shift herself to the table, best plates from the racks of the dresser, bone-handled cutlery, serving spoons, side plates, napkins; the lot. Eleanor brings the ham to the table on a platter and carves the pale meat in readiness. It flakes off the bone and she hands some to the boys to keep them going.

Everything in the kitchen is on the boil again: steaming puddings, poultry stock, spuds and cabbage, filling the kitchen with hissing and sighing. Spits of water spill over the rims of pots to form rolling balls on the hobs. By eight o'clock everything has boiled dry.

The boys sit next to each other at the far side of the table, their stomachs turning over, not solely down to the lack of food. Ellen sits by the range. Elizabeth snoozes on the settle, but whether she is pretending, Ellen can't tell. Eleanor paces the kitchen, pushing her hair back at the temples and stroking the fabric of her dress. She stands at the window looking out. *Bastard,* the boys hear her whisper under her breath.

It's stopped snowing now. The front has passed through and in its place stars dot the sky and a quarter moon hangs over the estuary. Everything looks brittle and sharp and clearly defined.

"You'd better go and look for him, boys. Yank him out and drag him home," she says, staring out over the yard. "I'll give you a crook," she laughs.

But she's not laughing really. The boys know that he's often late. It is the way things are. This is the shape of life at Mount Pleasant.

"Wrap up warm," their mother says, "don't want you catching your death. Got enough on my plate."

The boys take down their woven overcoats from the hooks at the side of the range, tie their mufflers around their necks, pull down their peaked caps, put on their woollen gloves, ready for the off. On the mat, under the lean-to outside the kitchen door, are placed their hob-nailed work boots, laces loose and yawning, just waiting to be stepped into.

"Don't hang around, d'you hear? Quick as you can," shouts their mother. "And close that door. You're letting all the heat out. Haven't got money to burn."

"We'd better get going. You heard what she said. Need to get a spurt on," says George.

Lantern in hand, Jack leads the way as George and he tread through the snow to the sheds where Salt and Pepper are barking in anticipation and straining at their leashes, running around in circles, chasing each other's tails.

"C'mon you two," says George, freeing them from the leash and ruffling their coats behind the ears. "Let's sniff the bugger out."

At first the dogs slink down on all fours at the shed door, muzzles on paws, eyeing the white stuff with suspicion.

"It's all right, boys. Won't harm," says Jack. "We'll take care of you."

The dogs nose the snow and – with their bellies grazing the surface – follow the sound of Jack's voice and his waiting hand.

"We won't take the gambo," says George. "Won't risk it. Just Celt."

"Aye. Makes sense if he's had a few too many. Save us trying to hold him up in all this," he says pointing at the yard where the cobbles are completely obscured by the snow.

George enters the stable and is met by the smell of hay and ammonia and warm dung.

"Sorry, boy. Going to have to go out in the cold. Duty calls."

Tonight he doesn't saddle up the old grey shire or take down the stirrups or the posh bridle with the fancy brasses. The plain leather one will do.

George cups his gloved hands at Celt's side and Jack places his boot in it before George gives him a leg up. The warmth of the gelding's back seeps through his inner thighs and his calves. He stretches out his torso so that it lies flat along the length of the horse's back, his face nestling into the mane which tickles his chin. For a few moments it makes him feel happy and unafraid, like being much younger again, free of responsibility. He breathes in the earthy smell of the poll, snuggles down, his arms wrapped around the withers, taking in the heat and the heart of his old friend.

Without a sound, the boys and animals leave the farm yard, Jack riding bare-back, George leading them, leather in one hand, lantern in the other, collies at the rear bursting with pent-up energy. As they climb the incline out of the village of Llanrhidian, Jack squeezes his thighs around Celt's girth to keep his balance. In the snow, with the familiar blotted out, he feels slightly disoriented and a little frightened up there, astride a seventeen-hand horse in the dark, looking for a drunken, stop-out father.

"We'll try the Greyhound first," says George as they halt for a minute at the cross at the top of the track.

"Aye. He's probably there," says Jack.

Back on the flat, Jack feels braver, soothed by Celt's sure-footedness through the snow, the dogs at heel, George leading the way. It's only a step to the Greyhound, a mile at most, on past the vicarage on the left, the parochial school on the right, on past Ebenezer and the wheelwright's, until the inn comes into sight.

"No sign of life," says George.

"Only idiots'll be out for a drink in this," says Jack.

"Well that's it though, isn't it?"

"Poor Mother."

"Poor us, more like. Selfish sod."

"Give it a try. Just in case. Perhaps he's in the back room. Or fallen asleep," says Jack.

George pushes through the snow with the dogs until he reaches the rear of the inn and raps on the window. Nothing. He tries the door. Hard. Insistent.

"All right. Keep it down," says the landlord answering the door, candle in hand.

"It's father. He hasn't come home," explains George.

"Well, what makes you think he's here?"

"Has he been in?"

"No. Not tonight. Christmas Eve, for God's sake. And only a fool would be out in this."

The words make his stomach turn over. How dare he call his father a fool. He knows it's true; but he doesn't have the right to say it. Not to his face.

"And?" asks Jack as George reappears with the lantern, shaking his head.

"No." says George.

"So it's the King's Head then, down with all those idiots in Llangenny."

"Another three miles. Bastard."

"No rush. Let's take our time. Have a bit of fun for once. It's Christmas."

"Mother's on pins. She made a big effort. And Ellen."

"It'll be all right."

"It's all right for you perched up there. Hard work this, so don't egg me on."

But Jack does egg his brother on, keeping on about pulling up Celt and taking time to have a bit of fun. They won't have this chance again. Tomorrow the snow will turn to slush and melt away as though it has never been.

So as they round the bend after the holloway at Stembridge, the sight that meets them at Burry Green weakens any resolve George has left after his brother ground him down. The duck pond is frozen over and blanketed with snow and the vast expanse of the village green now a white snowfield. Unmarked. Unspoiled. Bethesda and the minister's lime-washed house at the far end of the green shine out under the moonlight like a beacon.

"Be it on your head. Mother'll have your guts for garters as well as Father's for being so late," says George as Jack jumps off Celt and lands in the waiting cushion of snow to leave his mark.

He bends down and plunges his gloved fingers into the snow and rolls the flakes between his palms to form a ball.

"Fight?" he asks.

"You're on," says George as he makes a break and runs away from his brother as fast as the snow allows. He feels the snowball strike him on the back. He laughs and runs on, the cold air catching the back of his throat, the colour rising in his cheeks. He can't remember the last time he laughed like this, felt this free. He draws breath, stoops, makes his own snowball, large and firm and icy in his hands. He takes aim and throws overarm to score a perfect hit on Jack's chest. Jack falls to the ground, plays dead, stretching out his limbs like the points of a star. He closes his eyes, absorbing this new sensation of beautiful cold and softness.

George draws nearer. Lies down at his brother's side. For a few minutes the boys are together, matressed in snow looking up at the moon and the stars.

"Like magic, isn't it?" says Jack.

"Perfect," says George. "Could stay like this for ever."

But Salt and Pepper are nudging at their faces with their wet noses, tails wagging, wanting more chasing. And so the mock snowball fight starts again, and the dogs bark not knowing for sure whether it's a game or an assault that's taking place.

The boys are breathless now; but not tired and they are lost in the moments of the final hours of Christmas Eve.

"Just a half hour more," says Jack.

Just a half hour. Just as long as it takes for him to bury his brother in the snow, for him to cover him up completely, apart from his face, so he might always remember this night when the snow is gone. And for just as long as the time it takes for his brother to do the same for him so that he might feel the same sensation too. So that he will never forget it either. One after another they lie motionless on the snow while each

46

brother in turn scoops the snow and lays it on top of the other's body. They pat the snow firm, so that the body is buried in compacted crystals, like a sparkling quartz statue or a frozen figurine in a churchyard. But somehow they don't feel the cold or the passing of time.

So engrossed in fun are they that they don't notice that the dogs have run off. They can't see them anymore but they can hear barking. In the unruffled air, Pepper's yap is loud and shrill and Salt is joining in too, a lower, deeper bark. The boys can sense the urgency in the tone, painful and out of tune. It's coming from the direction of the Minister's House, there in the near distance, a couple of hundred yards ahead.

"We better make a move," says Jack. "Dad's missing."

"C'mon, boy," says George, taking Celt by the lead. "Walk on. Nice and steady now."

As they approach, the dogs bark louder. They're not playing anymore, not chasing their tails and circling, but padding back and fore, over and over the same patch of ground, the way their Mother often does in the kitchen back home.

In the ditch at the side of the track, near the chapel railings, there's a mound, partially covered with snow.

"Oh, God!" says George as he starts forward.

"Easy now, might not be," says Jack, pulling him back. "Take this a minute," he says handing him the lantern.

George holds out the lantern at arm's length as Jack bends, then kneels, to inspect the shape. George can feel his hand trembling; doesn't think he can keep it steady for long. And the cold has suddenly caught up with him.

The dogs are on their bellies now, heads down on the snow, eyes looking at Jack, wanting answers.

"Shhh, boys," says George as he rubs the collies behind the ears so that their tails begin to wag feebly. "Be all right."

Jack clears some of the snow from the mound. It doesn't take long to recognise the long, black coat, the heavy hob-nailed boots, the dark rimmed hat that has fallen off the head of thin grey hair. Jack reaches over and gently turns the body towards him and allows the light of the lamp to reveal the hollowed out face and the eyes still open. Like an abandoned sheep, their father lies in the frozen dirt, flakes of snow coating his body, his pewter hip flask beside him. Jack places his finger tips on the neck, feeling for a pulse, his lips to his father's lips, searching for the warm breath of life. He gets only the reek of rum.

"He's gone," says Jack.

"Too late, then," says George.

"Aye. Could have been here hours."

Where they get the strength from, they don't know, but together they heft the dead weight from the ditch and heave it across the waiting back of Celt, as they would a leather saddle. Their father's arms and legs hang down on either side like limp stirrups. And with the dogs quiet at their heels, they turn to head home without another word said in the bitterness of the winter's night.

Chapter 7

The boys turn into the yard and tether Celt to the post for the time being. Together they walk around the back, past the dairy and in through the kitchen door. They don't have to say anything: it's there in the stoop of the shoulders, the ashen faces, the scooped out eyes. It's as though their frozen clothes are the only things that are keeping them upright.

"Good God, no," says Eleanor.

She places her knitting on the chair and holds onto the solid oak arm.

Elizabeth rises from the settle and reaches for her walking stick to raise herself as best she can. She clutches the carved bone handle and taps her way across the quarry tiles to stand by her daughter-in-law. She threads her right arm through Eleanor's for support and rests her left hand on her stick. Eleanor feels Elizabeth's arm trembling and presses it into her body and then takes her right hand in hers and pats it over and over again.

Ellen feels her face pale as she rises from her chair to stand by her mother and grandmother.

The boys stand in their outdoor clothes, the warmth of the kitchen thawing the icy snow they've traipsed in with them.

It drips from their caps, their coats, the soles of their hob-nail boots so that they stand in miserable puddles of water in front of the range.

They walk toward the women to encircle them. They feel their mother's frame, taut and resistant in their arms, but their grandmother's body convulses and heaves to release a sound that they've only ever heard before in the sheds: the wail of a cow caught in a long and hard labour. It fills the kitchen, bouncing off its bare walls. It sounds as if it has been years in the making.

"That's it, Gran, let it out," says Jack. "Do you good. Do you good an' all, Mother."

"Don't you think I've done enough crying? Died a long time ago, as far as I'm concerned. Bring him in, boys. And then you'd better get out of those clothes or you'll catch your death as well."

The twins do not forget to remove their father's boots, as their mother insists, before they bring him back into the farm for the last time. They leave them outside the kitchen door, for the last time, uppers soaked through.

Ellen puts an arm around her mother and grandmother, stooping to one side, willing them to stay steady as they silently watch the twins struggle to carry William's body over their shoulders like a side of beef, across the kitchen, through the living room and up the narrow stairs towards the bedroom where he'd fathered them.

The boys feel – in the lifting and the heaving – the big man their father had once been. Tall. Big boned. Hands like spades.

They groan with the weight of those bones now, even though the flesh has fallen off them the last few years, the face sunk. Everything gone in on itself apart from the belly. That bloated tell-tale belly that was nothing to do with Mother's attempt to keep him alive with her cooking. He had just become a lesser sort of man in every way. It seemed he couldn't help it.

They manoeuvre William's frame up the final few treads and pause for breath on the landing before taking him into the front bedroom and placing him on the bed. They stand and look at him. Jack wonders if they'll follow him, what they'll turn out like in the end. They're not built like him. They're strong, yes; but are more like their mother, the Evans' side. Squatter. Stockier. Long in the waist and short in the leg. *Low-kneed* is Elizabeth's way of putting it. But their colouring is his as it was in his youth. Not this version, but the one with the dark wavy hair, the swarthy skin. And their eyes are his eyes too: brown, with hooded lids and slanting brows. Wicked, laughing eyes, their Mother used to say they were, once upon a time. Their ears too mark them as their father's sons: sticking out – like boxers' – with fleshy lobes.

"Remember when Ellen used to cut ribbon from Mother's knick-knack basket and wrap it round her head and under her chin?" says Jack, breaking his thoughts.

"Aye, flattening her ears to her head till they hurt."

"Least it shut her up for a while. But she still had those ears when she woke up in the morning."

They look once again at their father's ears and the small golden hoop piercing he has in his left lobe. They remember the tales he told them when they were young and he'd hold them, one on each knee, clutching them close. Sometimes he'd say he was the son of a travelling Gypsy who'd got lucky when he'd met Elizabeth. She'd stopped him roaming, settled him down in Gower where he'd bought the farm, acquired the fields, sired a strange and exotic son and called him William. The boys had never known their grandfather and when they'd pressed their father and Elizabeth for the truth, they'd only laugh and Elizabeth would say: *It's for us to know and you to find out.*

Other times he'd say said he was of noble blood and Spanish descent, a captain at sea who'd been washed ashore in Port Eynon and been blinded by love. Again they'd ask Elizabeth to corroborate; but all she'd say was: *Our lips iz sealed*, and they'd all laugh. The tales were endless: they'd loved the one about him being a sailor before he'd married their mother, a jolly tar who'd circumnavigated the world and crossed the equator more times than he could count on both hands. That's why he wore the earring, he'd say. To mark him out. It was his badge of honour.

And now they are old enough to understand the truth: that the earring was nothing more than a talisman, a lump of shiny metal worn in the hope of repelling demons and evil spirits that might enter his mind through his ear. A charm that might help his failing sight, stop him from going blind. A fat lot of good it did him in the end.

The women follow the young men slowly up the stairs, Elizabeth gripping the bannister with her right hand and levering herself up the treads with her left hand on her stick which points the way. They go into the bedroom, where the boys leave them to it.

Ellen sits down near the window and watches as her grandmother and mother begin their work. Slowly they take off her father's outer garments, his last show to the world, still soaked-through with the melted snow. They undo his tie, the tie which he never failed to wear – his last vestige of respectability – and then gently unfasten the studs of his shirt collar. His braces are next, which they slacken and slide slowly over his unresisting shoulders. His shirt is easier to unbutton and they do so, one by one, and undo his cuffs and throw the garment to the floor. The slow striptease of death. His woollen singlet underneath still hugs his emaciated body and they ease it over his lifeless head as nimbly as they can, before rolling down his long-johns without embarrassment. He lies there on his bed; naked, just as he'd been born, apart from the complexion of pale stillness.

As though from afar, Ellen observes the matriarchs doing the work of women. They dip their flannels in the bowl on the washstand and wipe his brow and lips free of the specks of earth. They remove his teeth for the time being. They take his hands, limp; her mother's hand wiping the right: her grandmother's, the left. They plug his orifices – including his *nether regions* as they called them – with lint and gauze and then put his teeth back in before tying a bandage under his chin around his head to keep his jaw tight. The laying-out complete, they dress him in his best winceyette nightshirt and ease him flat in the bed, snuggling the flannelette sheets up to his chin as if to tuck him in. They place copper pennies over his closed eyes and then kiss him and whisper *Goodnight.*

Ellen wonders what the women are thinking. They look capable enough, on the outside, their hands functioning automatically. Are they innately able to function like this at times of crisis? How strong they look. Ellen wonders if women are indeed stronger than men in some senses. But how strong are they in the face of their future? Would they ever survive without a man – any man – to lean on. They have never in their lives earned a penny from their own efforts and labours. Though she doesn't earn much, Ellen acknowledges that she likes the power and the independence it gives her. She is responsible for herself. That's good. It could have been so different. But now who will these women lean on?

Whatever her mother is thinking: there is no clue in her expression. *Don't show* is the motto they've always lived by at Mount Pleasant. There is just a tightness in her jaw as taut as the lifeless one she has just bandaged. In the glow of the candlelight, Ellen notices how dark the circles are under her mother's eyes, how hollow the cheeks. It is as if she is the shadowy corpse in the room. Perhaps she died a long time ago. All that washing and wiping couldn't really rinse the past. Ellen feels that her mother is no more than a collection of body parts, designed to please everyone except herself. Had she always been like that or is this what life here does to you in the end? With her father gone, her mother will now use those hands to cook and clean and carry for the twins, to cook and clean and carry for Ellen's grandmother, Elizabeth, until she can do it no longer. And then what? She dismisses the thought as soon as she realises what it might mean.

"I'm glad you were here, Ellen; all that way and you came."

"It's what I had to do, Mother," she replies.

Ellen feels her eyes welling as Elizabeth falls into a chair next to the washstand to get her breath back. Eleanor bundles up the discarded clothes that lie on the floorboards and starts to fold them and place them on a pile on top of the chest of drawers.

"Need to slow down maid," says Elizabeth, "Thee'll make thyself ill otherwise."

"You know me, Mother. Like to keep busy," she replies.

"Need to burn them all," says Elizabeth. "Boys'll see to it. No good to anyone now."

Eleanor stops what she's doing and strokes the top of the pile: the order she's attempting to make out of chaos. She picks off some of the bobbles of wool from the worn coat, a single strand of grey hair off the lapel. Then she takes the neck-tie from underneath the shirt and fondles it. The grey fabric is smooth against her ageing hands. She brings it up to her nose and breathes it in before sliding open the top drawer of the old chest and tucking it safely among their undergarments and night things.

"Sometimes death is the only cure, maid," says Elizabeth.

Eleanor ignores Elizabeth's adage.

"You're right. I'll get the boys to take these up the garden and burn them," she says, "I've got enough to take care of."

Chapter 8

The kitchen is still, but not silent after William comes home. The clock continues to tick, the cat continues to purr on the rug in front of the fire, and from her perch back on the settle in the corner come Elizabeth's intermittent gasps for air waking her from thick snores.

"Must have nodded off for a couple of minutes. Wasn't asleep though. Too tired for sleep," she says.

"Overtired. We all are," says Eleanor from her chair. "Hardly worth it anyway."

The twins sit facing each other across the table, Ellen at George's side waiting for first light. At the head of the table, William's empty carver chair looms larger this Christmas morning, its worn arms reaching out to the boys as if to grasp them and tug them into his old seat, absorb them into the very grain of the oak.

Eleanor knows what they are thinking so she talks out loud, on her own tack, making endless lists: *there'll be Doctor Matthews to call out as soon as we can; Hannah will need to know; Parson will have to be told – one of you boys will have to let him know after the service, I won't be going this morning with all I've got to do. We need to get a date before New Year for the funeral; Hezekiah Grove needs to come and measure up once today is over. And then once we get a date there'll be the food to sort. Flowers. Ellen, I'll need you for that. So, I don't need to spell it out. Can't sit around all day moping and talking to myself, not when there's work to be done.*

The rhythm of life at Mount Pleasant beats to the same tempo. Even though William is dead, even though it's Christmas Day, life goes on.

"No rest for the wicked," Elizabeth says as the twins go out the door.

Jack notices though that this morning her motto is not accompanied by the usual wink she gives with her left eye and the swivel of her head.

First, the yard needs to be shovelled, the front garden path cleared. The doctor will be coming as soon as he can. Then the heifers – they've led them from the lower pastures into the byres because of the storm – they'll need to be mucked out, given fresh hay, fed, talked to and stroked. The Jerseys need milking. There are lambing ewes to be checked in the fields up top, drifts of snow to be scoured for those who've sought shelter under the hedges. Swill to be fed to the sows in the piggery, dogs to be fed, horses to be brushed, brasses to be polished. When this is done, they'll need to scrub and polish themselves, get into their Sunday best, put on their black ties, their waistcoats, put their fobs and chains in their pockets and make themselves respectable to see the parson and call on the undertaker.

The women change into their mourning dresses ready to receive the long queue of callers. Eleanor paces the kitchen, constantly brushing down the pleats of her long black dress. The smell of camphor is strong in the air, nauseating on a sleepless stomach.

"You'll rub a hole in that if you're not careful," remarks Ellen.

"My insides are crawling," says Eleanor, "settle down once doctor's been. Be good to get it out of the way."

"Better keep a look out for him. Know what happened last time."

Eleanor goes through the little living room and out into the front porch to watch for Doctor Matthews in the lane. She doesn't under any circumstances want him coming across the yard and in through the back kitchen. She stands at the door to ensure he comes in through the garden gate, along the cleared path to the front door. Away from the geese.

That had been an early morning call too. William had gone down to the doctor's house next to the mill at the bottom of the village to get him urgently. George had been a baby then. Woken with the croup in the early hours. The cold, probably. Eleanor remembers how the curtains in the twins' bedroom had been stuck to the inside of the window when she and William had gone in. William was attuned to their cries as much as she was. More so, perhaps, since the first George and the accident. Jack had slept through the lot: the rasping on the in-breath, the barking on the out, the wheeze of the stridor. He'd always had trouble with his chest, George.

Could tell him and Jack apart by the coughing if you didn't know them.

She'd lifted George from the bed and carried him downstairs to the kitchen, filled the kettle and waited impatiently for it to come to the boil. The steam had filled the room as she'd wrapped him in a shawl Welsh-fashion, willing the droplets of moisture to break the cough. William couldn't stand to listen to him; and when dawn broke, but not the cough, he'd gone for Doctor Matthews.

He'd come later to the back door, bleeding from the back of his knee, and cursing the damned geese. *They've only gone and pecked my varicose vein*, he ranted. William had taken a towel and pressed it firmly to the wound until the bleeding stemmed. They could hardly help themselves from laughing, even though little George was struggling. And then he'd taken his stethoscope out of his bag, listened to the little boy's chest and said, *He'll live. Don't know about me, though.*

There'd been perfect little red-round circles on George's cheeks, the size of half crowns, before they got the temperature down. They'd held tepid flannels to his temple and then immersed his little body in a bowl of warm water on the kitchen table, William stirring the water gently with his great big hands. After the doctor left, he concocted a hot drink of honey and lemon and sat George on his lap, making him sip the cure off a silver teaspoon, his Christening spoon.

From the step of the front door, she watches as the doctor comes along the path. He seems to have shrunk from the man he once was, his frame stooping with the weight of the years.

Old Doctor Matthews – who'd once been known as Young Doctor Matthews when he first came to the village. His eyes meet hers; keen, warm eyes that are just as bright, but now sunken. Deeply etched laughter lines frame those eyes and as he draws close, she feels compelled to work out if it's true that every one of those lines marks a decade, as the concentric rings of an oak trunk mark each single year. She makes the tally seven. That can't be, surely.

All the years between then and now come into focus there on the threshold. He's been good to her and the family over the decades, comforted them through the times following the death of the first George, been there at the births of all her children. She'll never forget the Wednesday in March when he dragged Ellen screaming into the world with the aid of metal tongs. There had been impressions left on her temples which faded over the months, but the yelling had always persisted. *You're going to have trouble with that one,* he'd said with a smile. *Wednesday's child is full of woe. Good luck!* Where did the years go?

She shakes his hand and brings him into the passage and up the stairs to the bedroom. She looks at William's body, for a moment expecting to see his chest rise and fall, for him to open his eyes, perhaps smile at her. She is sure that the bristles on his chin and cheeks have poked through overnight. But he is as still as only death can be.

"Wasn't as though we weren't expecting it, Eleanor, was it?" says Doctor Matthews.

"No. But I always hoped," says Eleanor. "And to go like this. Dead in a ditch...."

"I know. But I doubt if he suffered much – at least at the end."

Doctor Matthews takes out his fountain pen from his leather bag and records the official cause of death as *hypothermia* in his familiar scritchy-scratchy writing in black ink. The finality of the form and the signature hits hard as Eleanor puts out her hand to take the certificate from the doctor there in the soft, intimate space of the bedroom.

Back downstairs, Eleanor instructs the family what to say when people from the village start to call at Mount Pleasant with their condolences, as they would, one after the other, uttering: *Sorry for your loss.*

"Peacefully, in his sleep, in his own bed, at home with his family, that's what you say, you hear?" she tells them.

The next day, the parson calls and a date is set for the funeral. Despite it being a busy time, he can fit it in before the New Year, he says.

The day after Boxing Day, Hezekiah Grove, the village carpenter and coffin-maker comes to measure-up. *Nothing but the best*, says Eleanor, *I've put a bit by.*

In the parlour that's kept for show, Eleanor and Ellen spend what's left of the day down on their hands and knees with a dustpan and broom. Eleanor is in charge of operations. Nowhere is a speck of dust allowed to settle. The rugs are taken outside and put over the line and beaten to one inch of their lives, then put back down over the scrubbed tiles. The cushions are plumped and arranged and then re-arranged. The lustre jugs on the dresser are wiped, the furniture rubbed until it gleams. The fire is left laid but not lit. The curtains are drawn both back and front.

By the early evening of December 28th, fifty-eight-year-old William Thomas lies in a fine oak coffin on a wooden trestle. He is ready to be viewed, open to the world, couched in white silk and dressed in his best suit, though it hasn't fitted him for a long time. His large calloused hands are crossed at his chest, and Eleanor has insisted his signet ring stays on. His eyes are closed now and his grey hair combed. Eleanor has made sure that his earring stays, too. He is surrounded by white chrysanthemums that she has picked from the greenhouse he allowed her space for at the side of his veg plots in the allotment. Their perfume melds with beeswax and the strong odour of the four tallow candles burning on the mantle. It makes for a strange and potent mix.

They will come in their scores from the village to Mount Pleasant to pay their respects. They will come from all over the peninsula, north and south. William and Eleanor's daughter, Hannah will come from the pub in Loughor with her husband Charlie and the baby in her belly.

Chapter 9

Cold dead inside; dead cold outside. Ellen stands at the kitchen window gazing out southwards through the thin pane of glass that struggles to separate these two frozen worlds. It has been icy cold since the night William died but there is now only a little while longer for him to lie shrouded in the chill of the front parlour. Where is the thaw George has predicted?

Ellen hopes it will come soon. The last thing she wants today is one of her wretched headaches. Already the jagged zigzags have started their splintery dance in front of her eyes. Probably the reflected light off the snow – too white, too bright. Snowflakes on the outside of the glass have created an almost perfect symmetry with her grandmother's crochet centre-piece and her mother's doilies, glinting in the sun on the table-top.

The twins are outside working, trying to finish up ready for the funeral. It is rare for her to be alone in the kitchen in the muffled silence. Funny how preparing for a wake is not that different from preparing for a wedding breakfast, she thinks. The wedding breakfast that might have been if things had been different, her wedding breakfast that everyone thought would happen, that everyone had just taken for granted. She presses her warm nose to the window pane and breathes – hot live breath – onto the cold surface and watches the droplets moisten the glass. She finds her fingertip tracing initials in the moisture: RT and ET. She watches her index finger reveal their initials once again, Richard Tucker's connection with her made momentarily real again in condensation. She wonders if a more permanent mark of their relationship is still visible on the limestone slabs at the top of the hill behind the house. She recalls them scratching their initials with stones into a crude heart with an arrow piercing it straight through the centre. He hadn't laughed when she'd teased him with one of her mother's adages:

Change the name and not the letter
Change for worse and not for better.

With the sleeve of her dress, she wipes ghosts of the past that have begun to whisper—

"Ellen? Ellen? Give me a hand with this, will you?"

Eleanor. The memory and emotions are stale and rotten in any case. Ellen takes one corner of the damask cloth; her mother, the other. Was it only a few days ago they'd done this in readiness for Christmas? Separated by acres of floating cloth, as white as the fields outside, they drape it over the kitchen table. No thaw expected here. The snap and crack of words on their tongues; some that would be spoken; others left unsaid.

"Changed your mind, then, Mother?" asks Ellen.

"No. And I won't be, either, despite you going on. Not done," replies her mother.

"What d'you mean, 'not done'?"

"Listen, Ellen, don't take that tone with me. You know what it's like – women just don't do it – not their place."

"Place? What on earth are you talking about?" says Ellen, her voice rising, her cheeks reddening. "I just don't see it like you do."

"Nor me," comes the voice from the settle.

"See, Mother."

Ellen takes a perverse delight whenever her grandmother speaks up for her against her mother. A good ally. Didn't *waste words*, as she put it, but they were always there at the right time to create maximum impact.

"Right. You've had your say, both of you and I don't know why *she's* putting her two-penny worth in. *She* won't be going either. As for you, Ellen; do as you feel fit. But my face won't be shown outside this door today, and that's final."

"Have it your way, then," says Ellen.

"I will," says Eleanor. "Now we need to get cracking. Don't want to show poor."

Ellen breathes out audibly. Elizabeth gives her the thumbs up from afar.

"Got more to think about, I'm sure, than our cups and saucers," she scoffs.

"That's what you might think," retorts Eleanor.

"Can't be bothered myself. Enough to be going on with here don't you think?"

"Got a lot to learn, my girl. Just you wait and see. So," she adds emphatically, "it'll be the best china and the best spread we can lay on. Still got my pride if nothing else."

And with that torrent Eleanor stills and Ellen and Elizabeth know better than to say anything in reply.

For the next three hours the three women knead, flour-deep in dough and roll the pastry and bake the bread. There will be apple tarts and mince pies; bara brith and teisen lap and Welsh cakes flipped on the maen. They take down the ham from the charnel and slice it thick, no scrimping – there'd be lashings of it. The table would be groaning under the weight of the spread after the burial.

Chapter 10

It is just a couple of hundred yards from Mount Pleasant to the church dedicated to the two saints of St. Illtyd and St. Rhidian, all downhill along the narrow track slicing through the village green. William's body would be carried rather than be horse-drawn. They'd done that for the first George and they'd do it for William too.

The six coffin-bearers assemble themselves in the parlour in readiness for the achingly heavy task. Hannah's husband, Charlie Redding, who has – surprisingly, for a publican, Eleanor said – done the right thing, takes up the rear along with Towzer, the local blacksmith. The twins have commandeered two local lads, Brawn and Beef, to go in the middle, and they position themselves at the front.

Jack gives the instructions and – at the count of three – all the bearers bend their knees ready to heave the oak casket up on to their shoulders. They groan as they strain to straighten up. Taking tiny, choreographed steps like trained dancers, their polished black shoes shuffle out into the narrow passage and into the front porch. Eleanor has made it clear that William will leave his house for the final time through the front door.

First in line behind the coffin, Ellen heads the mourners:

close family and friends who already gathered in the house earlier for a private service with the parson, and whose number will be swelled by those lining the route.

The thaw has come by now, just as George has predicted. Spot-on again, thinks Ellen. Country lore. Probably in the blood. As for her, she already wishes it had stayed dry for now it is tamping down, leaden-grey curtains of it. Perfect funeral weather. Even before she rounds the bend from the farm lane to the top of the village, she is drenched, her hair a mess, strands straggling from under her black hat. Bloody rain! What will she look like?

She faces the village green. Good God – a sea of mourning-black. They've all crawled out of their individual holes from the far-flung corners of the peninsula, hundreds of them. Always brings them out, a funeral of one of their lot. Gives them a chance to get together, all these sad, solitary little men, to pay their respects, give a good send-off. Or is it perhaps a reconnaissance exercise? Are they thinking, let's have a look at what kind of a turn-out William Thomas gets. But what they really mean is, what sort of a turn-out am I going to get when my turn comes? How will I compare?

Look at them, standing there, their hats in their hands; an apocalyptic vision in the silence save only for the incessant beating of the rain on the canopies of their black umbrellas as they gawp and wait for the cortège to file past.

Ellen breathes in the scene. Just as she expected. Men; just men. Nothing changes. They seem as though they've been set down in this peninsula along with the old red sandstone.

Shoulder-to-shoulder, three deep, they stand along the route, though Ellen can only see the ones at the front. In their Sunday best, they all look the same. Brynley Evans, Meadow Bank. He was old when she left. Didn't think he could possibly still be alive. Always was an old fossil. Hardly worth him going home after the funeral. *Your turn next, Brynley*, she feels like shouting. And Joseph Jenkins, Barrastone Hall Farm – must be ninety if he's a day. How is it possible for a man to be so hunched and still walk? But he has a gnarly old stick; just like him, miserable old bugger. Father wouldn't want *him* here, that's for sure.

Ellen takes them all in. Mother'll want to know who turned out. Want a list so she'll better get it right! Well, there's Ellis Taylor, Penymynydd. No good boyo – one of the gambling set. That'll get Mother's goat up. How on earth Gwen still puts up with him, she'll never know. Twenty–five years engaged and still no commitment. Says he's not ready to settle down, just yet. Keeps buying her earrings and necklaces and bangles. Buying time. She says they're diamonds; Mother says they're paste. Ellen doesn't care what they are. Nothing would ever buy her off. She'll never be traded again.

On his right is Edward Morgan, from Crichton. Face like a crater and a broken nose with a scar that runs down the ridge and across his cheek and over his lips. Used to be handsome, they say, before he got kicked in the face by the spooked yearling. Still a bit of a ladies' man, by all accounts.

And the young saplings have turned out too: a whole tribe of Reeses from Cae Forgan: five almost identical but damaged peas in a pod. Father said they shared a brain. Put it down to old man Rees marrying Ada Bevan, his first cousin. Turned out well, though. Five faces scrubbed, soapy clean and polished like saucepans after a good going-over.

She gets the sudden urge to laugh as her eyes go back to the cortège in front of her. From behind they look like the twelve legs of a pantomime horse, shuffling along under the heavy weight. And those suits. The same ones they've been wearing since she upped sticks and left: too tight at the waist, too short at the arms, too short in the leg, ankles showing and none of them thoroughbreds. She holds herself in check and adopts a demeanour more in keeping for a daughter in mourning.

Ellen passes all the mourners, her eyes fixed on the church ahead, though she can still feel their penetrating eyes boring into her, long after. A woman on her own. How dare she? What is it with the church and its rules? Why do women always do as they think they should, not as they wish?

The bell tolls in the Norman stone church tower, reverberating in the stillness which is suddenly splintered by the parson's voice, booming with conviction:

He that believeth in me, though he were dead, yet shall he live and whosoever liveth and believeth in me shall never die.

Ellen takes her place at the front, in a pew in the nave. She can't for the life of her fathom why religion has to feel so uncomfortable. Cold air; hard seats; lime-peeling walls. Even with the new roof – wonder who's paid for that? – it is still freezing. She slides her bottom across the polished wooden surface, unable to settle. She feels small and insignificant, just one mortal soul of hundreds who sat here over the centuries; but also conspicuous, wedged uneasily between the family mourners, a single black skirt in a press of suits.

She tries to make eye contact with her brothers, see how they're bearing up. But they're facing the altar, acting like the good boys they can be on occasion. She wonders if they'll let their hair down later, once the beer starts to flow. Wonders if there'll be any fights. She hasn't forgotten about Gower funerals.

On and on the parson's voice drones in that monotonous ecclesiastical way. She yawns; a wide, cavernous gape, which she attempts to stifle with her gloved hand. Try as she might, she finds it hard to maintain her concentration on hearing messages she isn't convinced by – though she loves the poetry of the words, simple and clear, just as it is simple and clear that she loved her father despite everything. After all, she was of his blood, as they say in these parts.

At long last the event is nearly over and the family begins the slow trek behind the coffin out through the church, so full that men cram the aisle at the back, near the gallery. So many pairs of eyes; eyes she can't put faces to at that moment. And on out into the yard and up the path to the Thomas family grave. She watches as her father is lowered into the waiting chasm, the freshly dug soil piled high at the side. It doesn't seem any time since those dark months following the first George's death when her father would feel compelled to come down to this grave. Those heavy, rain-drenched days when he'd say to her mother: *Can't bear to think of that boy alone down there, getting wet-through*. Poor Father. Her dear tortured father who'd never forgiven himself for that day when the heifers had stampeded. Can be with the first George now, look after him again, she thinks. There, at the graveside, she wonders where her resting place would be too, when her time came; where she'd *feel comfortable* being buried, as her owl-wise grandmother puts it.

She slips away from the graveside, the rain still teeming, her boots sinking into the newly churned mud. Arm in arm with her twin brothers, she leads the way to the lych gate where she takes her place and waits to receive, and to accept, with the shake of a hand and a tearless eye, the condolences offered directly to her. They're waiting there, a snake of black-coated mourners, anonymous from a distance; waiting their turn to file past.

She feels him before she sees him. He is with his father, Matthias, next in the queue. Two years. Now here he is. Keep calm, she tells herself. Act normally. What is normal anyway when you just buried your father?

Her attention drifts from the people talking to her, their *so sorry to hear* and *be strong for your family* now jarring and discordant. She wants to run. Don't be ridiculous, that's not protocol. Anyway, why run? It's not you that needs to be running. Just keep calm. The trembling's down to the grief – it's been a long few days – it's been a terrible shock – you're exhausted, emotionally wrung-out. Death is a tiring business.

She feels her hands, quivering and clammy under her black gloves. Her heart races. Her mouth is dry. That headache will be next.

"Nell, I'm really sorry about your father, please accept my condolences."

Richard. His voice is hesitant and gentle as he takes her hands in his and holds them there for perhaps longer than is required.

Ellen inhales again, deeply. Mustn't show.

"Thank you, Richard. Very kind of you. Would have meant a lot, you coming like this. And you too, Matthias," she adds, addressing Richard's father, who waits his turn. "And you're both more than welcome to come back to the house."

What is she saying? Welcome? These two? Do the right thing, Ellen, just for today... for the family. But it is Matthias's words that echo down the years. Those gut-wrenching words she overheard as she stood in the sitting room, addressing her father in the kitchen: *Look, William, it cannot be.*

Chapter 11

The rain is relentless, a monotonous tamping on the timber roof of the lych gate, cascading off the eaves onto the path. All the mourners have already passed through and now Ellen and the twins are bunched up on the covered bench inside, waiting in the futile hope of the downpour easing. Being there for just a little longer gives her breathing space to get herself together before going back to the farm.

"Did well there, sis," says Jack. "Bloody nerve of them."

"You don't think he saw me shaking, then?" she asks. "Heard it in my voice?"

"Not the slightest tremor. Got to give it to you. Bloody good actress," says George.

"Mmm," she says. "Need to keep up the role for another hour or so yet, though."

"We'll keep him talking. And that old man of his. Not to worry," says Jack.

"Right. Better be making tracks," says George. "Know what she's like. Think we've stopped off for a quick one."

"Could do with a pint, mind," says Jack. "Hell of a thirst on me. Few of them have stopped off in the Welcome, I see..."

"Aye, didn't even bother to shake hands. Slunk out the other way, across the churchyard, over the stile, and straight into the Dolphin through the back garden."

"Pious farts," says Ellen. "Worst of the lot, church-goers."

"And she was here, too. Did you see her? Esther the Cats? Disappeared like a puff of wind," says Jack.

"Don't, Jack. She gives me the creeps. Always has. That long black coat of hers, that pulled-down hat, that funny old walking stick, the hob-nailed boots. Strange little woman living up there all alone, like that. Never heard her say a word. Ever. But somehow she's always there: funerals, weddings, christenings. Standing distant and alone seeing everything from afar," says Ellen thoughtfully.

"She's all right," says George, "no harm in her. Just different, that's all."

Ellen wonders for a moment if that's why Esther gives her the chilling feeling: will she herself be the strange little woman living somewhere all alone one day? An outsider living on the edge of things, in a long black coat? So there were two women at the funeral after all, she realises: two women in a press of trousers. Why was Esther alone like this? What's made her an outsider and a figure of fun, a presage of doom in her own village? She never thought about it until now. Not really. And she'll never go close enough to Esther to search out the answers.

"How many cats she got now?" asks Ellen. "Can you imagine that coat of hers? That house in the woods?"

"They're all she's got," says George. "Company."

Ellen wonders if cats are the only company she'll keep one day.

"Witch, if you ask me," she says. "Makes me shiver."

"Aye," says Jack, "remember when the three of us used to go out under the hill and knock her door at The Laurels and then run like hell, George's chest wheezing like an accordion?"

"Knew it was us though, didn't she? Knows everything. Perhaps even the future," says Ellen. "C'mon. Let's go. I can feel her, still. Goose-bumps all over."

George opens his large umbrella and he and Jack tuck their sister between them, linking arms as they walk slowly, with heavy steps, up the steep slope back to Mount Pleasant. Under the black canopy, shielded from the world, they take a few moments' respite from the rain and the emotional drain of the last few days.

As they approach the lane to the farmhouse, Ellen sees that the curtains that Eleanor has drawn since William died, are open again at the front. Funny how the simple swish of some fabric can indicate so much, how time is already passing.

Eleanor has warned them that, today, they come in through the front door. *Way it's done,* she said. And so it's the warmth that hits Ellen as she enters the house and into the passage: open fires are alight in the parlour and the little living room off the kitchen, which functions as a second-best room. Sometimes William used to use it as an office before things got on top of him and the bills piled up on the metal spike on the desk. But all that has been tidied up, locked inside the cupboard underneath the sloping writing surface; for today, at least.

There are men in black everywhere, spilling out of the parlour and the living room into the passage, holding their hats under their arms and cups of tea in their hands. They talk together in mean little huddles. About her father, probably. About what's going to become of the farm and the family now he's gone. About the feuding and the farmers he's in debt to, owes land to. Two-faced hypocrites, coming into his house, stepping over his threshold, accepting his widow's hard-won hospitality. Say it out loud, she wants to scream. Go on. Say it to my face, you white-whiskered, holier than thou, vipers. Call yourself Christians?

The conversation ceases as Ellen passes through and smiles graciously. They nod their heads in acknowledgement. Why is gossiping seen to be the prerogative of women, she wonders as she looks at their little cliques, imagining their sniping and back-biting and their filthy muck-spreading. As they stand there, drying out, off them comes the smell of drenched outer garments, with stale tobacco and pipe-smoke impregnated in the fabric. They must have been out in the garden for a quick smoke, as Eleanor would under no circumstances allow smoking inside Mount Pleasant. What with all the upset and anticipation of the encounter with Richard and Matthias, Ellen feels sick to her stomach.

She removes her coat and hat, and hangs them on the mahogany stand. She glances in the little mirror among the pegs and smooths down her black dress and attempts to tidy up her hair. No sign of him as yet, though. Logically, her head tells her coldly that she has no wish to talk to him. But her gut is signalling something other. She feels she is all liquid, her insides like the buttermilk swishing in the churn in the dairy, and a rancid burning sensation repeating in her throat, like milk on the turn. But her feet walk her automatically towards the kitchen where she senses he'll be.

Her mother catches her eye as she comes in the door to forewarn her. She breathes in, holds the breath, sucks in her abdomen, makes herself taller, as she heads for the refuge of the settle in the corner. Her grandmother smiles that smile of hers and pats the seat, beckoning her to join her. Ellen feels safe here with Elizabeth. She might have crossed the Atlantic twice on her own, and carved out a new life in amongst strangers six thousand miles away, but this afternoon, here on her own territory, in her own kitchen, she feels like a little girl again.

"Come and have a cwtch, maid. You look all in," says Elizabeth.

And she leans her head against her grandmother and comforts herself by inhaling the old smell of the little black crocheted shawl. Elizabeth has it draped around her broad shoulders that continue to support her without one word of complaint. Ellen unconsciously weaves her fingers through the holes between the wool.

"You still hankering? Still carrying a torch for that one?" Elizabeth asks as they both look across to the far side, near the kitchen door, where Jack and George are deep in conversation with Richard and Matthias, just as they'd vowed they'd be.

"Don't be daft, Gran. After what those two did?" says Ellen.

"Good. Bad blood, that Tucker lot."

From the island of the settle, Ellen feels like an outsider, an observer of a strange scene in a faraway country she has lost touch with. Isolated. Apart from family, Jack's Annie is the only woman there, following Eleanor around like a puppy in training, awaiting instruction, eager to please. Little Annie Beynon. Not so little now, younger than Ellen yet older than Jack. He'd always had a soft spot for her, freckle-filled face. Shoulder-length russet hair with a big green bow. Sun slanting through the window as Ellen and Annie, the children they were, sat in the double-oak desk in the village school, puzzling over their arithmetic. Chalk on slate. Giggling. Shhhh now, Mr. Jenkins might hear. Who'd have thought? Annie Beynon, and her Jack. Ellen's smile is bitter-sweet. A smile that says: *so life will go on at the farm.* A smile that says: *Annie Beynon will make a good wife, just like Mother. Bred for purpose.*

At the table, feeding her face with cake and pastries, sits her elder sister Hannah, obviously very fit for purpose. Her swollen belly is battling to conceal itself under her shabby coat, the buttons at the point of bursting with the struggle to contain the heavy hips, the thickening waist, the ever-engorging breasts with the spider-blue veins and the brown nipples that will soon gush milk for the baby who will suck her dry. Perhaps suck the very life out of her. Or perhaps not. She looks happy. But you could never tell with Hannah.

Ellen looks at Richard, so shy and at odds with his father, who is loud and animated, mandibles well oiled, chuntering on nineteen to the dozen. No wonder old Matthias was known as Jaws Tucker. Never ran out of words. Probably boring her brothers to death as they pretend to listen to him, those sticky-out ears of theirs on high alert. Talk about mart or some agricultural fair or other, no doubt. About stock. Buying and selling. Or how they've put a prize bull to one of their heifers, or a ram to an old ewe. But they wouldn't be talking about her. *You'll make fine breeding stock,* Richard had once joked with her. *I love a big-hipped woman. You'll pop out sons like peas.*

That's when she'd had to tell him that it probably wouldn't be. It was already eighteen months they were walking out together when she finally plucked up courage to reveal to him that it would be unlikely that she'd ever be able to bear him children, leave alone sons. That was when everything started to come undone, like the outgrown pullovers her mother would unravel, stitch by stitch, row by row, when she was a child. She'd be sitting on the little wooden milking stool her father made her, planted firmly between her mother's legs as Eleanor wrapped the crinkled wool around her waiting outstretched finger to form skeins. Wool that would come in handy, ready to be used again, some other time.

Her mother catches her eye again. This time it's with one of her looks which means, *Don't just sit there in the corner. Don't be rude. And don't show!*

She doesn't feel like talking and she knows that one of her headaches is well on the way. She can see little white floaters in front of both eyes, feel a tingling sensation in her left cheek and down that whole side of her body. Knowing that it's *only a migraine* doesn't make it any easier to bear. It's been building all day: the peculiar aura, which she thought might have been down to Esther the cats, has now intensified; and there's a throbbing in her temples, the pound, pound, pound of it keeping time with the pound, pound, pound of her heart.

She was so frightened when it first happened. She was about thirteen. Her mother put it down to her 'growing up' and turning into a woman. But she didn't turn into a woman in her mother's sense of the word but lost her vision temporarily, was violently sick, and her limbs ceased to function. Her mother, worried that she'd had a stroke, had called Young Dr. Matthews to the house. He found her in the bedroom, curtains pulled tight as the light was intolerable. Every time she tried to raise her head from the pillow, she was sick into the chamber pot.

She can smell the stench now in her nostrils. The acidity. Can hear Doctor Matthews words booming down years: *She'll probably grow out of it. Tension, you know.* And her mother's, too: *You told me she'd be a handful when she was born. The forceps, remember? Headstrong, she is. Needs to calm down a bit. Learn to relax.* He was wrong. But as for her mother, she hates to admit; she was right.

She's all of a work now. Struggling to keep herself together. She will not let it show.

She walks slowly to join Hannah at the table, giving the appearance of aloofness and haughtiness as she holds her head high and still. No one knows that with every step, drums are banging inside her skull, her teeth have high pitched sensations running through them. Her gums ache. Her jaw is tight. She wonders if anyone can tell how difficult it is for her to form words, to wrap her numbing tongue around the syllables?

"How many are you eating for?" she asks in what seems to her a monotone. "Not twins, is it? Run in families, you know."

"Hope not. Couldn't stand that. Just starving all the time. Sweet things, mostly," Hannah says reaching for another slice of bara brith and spreading it thickly with butter. "D'you make this?" she goes on. "Lovely. Why don't you have some?"

"Not hungry. Headache," Ellen says, gagging. "A blinder."

"Him over there, most likely. Why is he here? And Matthias. How they've got the nerve to put their faces in after how they treated you, I'll never know."

"I asked them," says Ellen. "Just came out."

"You and your mouth. Have you spoken to him? You know, *spoken* to him?"

"Only at the churchyard. Pleasantries, that's all," says Ellen.

"You need to let him have it. Don't hold back. Treat you like that. Like an animal. Not like you to hold your tongue."

"Leave it now, Hannah. Don't let's waste any more time. Tell me, how's Loughor?"

Ellen puts her listening face on and her hand under her chin as Hannah begins to tell her how excited she is about the coming baby. How excited they both are, her and Charlie. It's not ideal, she knows, bringing a baby into the world at the back of a pub, but they're going to do the best they can. They've got a few bits and pieces ready, a little crib and blankets and matinee coats and bonnets that Charlie's mother

82

has knitted. Ellen's eyes are staring straight though her sister's face as she talks on and on about the coming child without drawing breath, her lips opening and closing until Ellen wants to seize them between her fingers and squeeze them shut, for her to be still and silent. She listens to her drone on with her antennae fixed somewhere beyond Hannah, trying to pick up on Richard and the much-missed lilt of his voice.

"Of course, Charlie's even more worried now about the pub, with the baby on the way," says Hannah, causing Ellen to re-focus.

"Worried? Why? Thought the pub was doing well," says Ellen.

"Well, that's just it. Trade's right down. Half of what it was this time last year," she explains.

"I don't understand. Mines. Factories. All those thirsty hulks wanting to come to the trough after a day's work."

"They're not so thirsty now. Not for ale, anyway," she says. "Not in Loughor."

"What, then?"

"God. That's what they're thirsty for. Taking its toll on the pub since that man got them going."

"What man?" asks Ellen.

"I know you've been in America, Ellen, but you can't *not* have heard? Evan Roberts. Raging through Wales like an inferno, he is. Flames licking a long way further than Loughor with his preaching and his calling for souls."

"Boys haven't said anything," says Ellen.

"Well, they've been up to their eyes in it. They would have, otherwise. And they will," she says. "Miner, he was. Loughor boy. Only twenty-six. Don't know him, do you? Fine-looking man, they say. Charismatic. Anyway, got the nod from above to get one hundred and fifty thousand souls and he's well on his way. Preaching all around here. Meeting halls, chapels, outside the mines. Goes on till four in the morning, I've heard. We should go. See what he's made of."

"In your condition?" says Ellen.

"Why not?"

"Yes, why not? Though he'll be wasting his time with me. Let things settle down and then we'll go. The boys. Annie. You. Me. Give me something to take my mind off things."

"Look, don't let on to Mother about the pub or anything. She's got enough to worry about, all the mess to sort out. She's going to drop like a stone once all this is over. Between you and me, right?"

"Promise," says Ellen.

"And don't be in a rush to end up like me," she says. "Not everything, you know – marriage, babies. Not all it's cracked up to be."

And with that, Ellen excuses herself quickly from Hannah. She feels the room losing its shape. Verticals and horizontals are becoming distorted; the floor rising in front of her eyes. She needs air. She steadies herself, one hand on the table, and rises to make her way to the back door.

This time it's Richard who catches her eye. He's seen that pallor before, can read what's about to happen by her colour, the change from olive to vanilla. Her eyes: the pupils dilated so that they blacken the already dark brown irises, dark circles shadowing the hollows below her lower lids. He opens the kitchen door for her as she rushes past him, her skirt brushing his trouser leg in her haste. He doesn't follow her out of the door, up the stone steps into the allotment, but closes it quietly behind her. He'll give her time.

It's still raining but she doesn't care. She likes the feel of the water on her hair, on her cheeks, soaking into her thick, stifling dress. It's a baptism of sorts. William's snawl is where he left it, dug firmly into the far end of the veg plot, just out of sight from the kitchen. Sets of onions are coming through green and fresh in neat rows. She clings on to the long wooden handle to steady herself as she heaves into the damp earth. Not what her father would have wanted, her retching like this, she knows. There is something of a release about vomiting, a purging of body and soul when you have felt sick for too long. Despite the nausea and the migraine, she puts her back into digging into the soil with the snawl. The sharp metal edge cuts through the earth, which she lets fall over the contents of her stomach, to leave no trace, as if it had never happened.

She pulls herself back to an upright position and wipes her brow with her handkerchief. She's sweating as well as wet. She blows her nose hard until the burning smell of the vomit is gone. With her handkerchief, she dabs her mouth with some of her spittle just as her mother used to do to her when she was young. With both hands, she cups her nose and mouth to be affronted with the stench of her own breath. And then at the top of the steps, him.

Chapter 12

The new year announces itself with a sharp frost and clear skies. The sun is low, and out over the estuary the winter-blue sky is delineated from the blue-grey sea by the horizon that could have been drawn with a steel edge. Everything looks fresh, up close and in focus in this northern glinting January light: an empty canvas ready to be painted on.

It's a pity then that the strikes of the kitchen clock that counted the old year out did nothing to quell the anxiety, end the long spell of depression that seemed to be smothering the farm like a too-heavy winter carthen.

Distorted by a hangover, William's shadow looms large across the kitchen wall, much larger than in real life to the twins this morning. They're yet to learn of the long-term legacy, the consequences of his disintegration, his degradation. They sit at the table, still maudlin in their cups, knowing that they need to get cracking: the stock has no capacity to understand that it's New Year's Day, their stomachs can't wait. They wish they hadn't got up to their old pranks. Seems so out of place now, so mis-timed.

"You look worse for wear," says Ellen as she comes into the kitchen, her voice too loud, knocking against their skulls. "What time did you get in?"

"Three," says George, "perhaps later. D'you have to be so shrill?"

"Thick head, have we? Serves you right. Think you'd know by now," she says.

"Seemed all right at the time," says Jack. "Never again."

"How many times have I heard that? You're not going to get any sympathy from Mother so don't just sit there waiting to be fed like the cattle or that stupid cat there. Suggest you get out and work it off. Get from under her feet before she comes down. But, fill me in: just where did you get to last night?"

"It was his fault," says George. "Talked me into doing the rounds with the Mari Lwyd. Us and Beef and Brawn. And now my chest is off again. Tight as hell."

Ellen pours herself a cup of tea, elbows on the table, chin in her palms, all ears.

"Well," says George, "we'd gone down the Dolphin for a quick one. Not stopping, we'd said. But after the first couple of pints had slid down without touching the sides, I suppose we changed our minds a bit, didn't we, Jack?"

"Aye, we did," grunts Jack.

"Anyway," George goes on, "all the village boys were in there, Towzer, Gringo, and like I said, Beef and Brawn. Playing skittles, they were. Just after eleven, him there – clever-dick, Jack – says, 'How about we do the rounds with the Mari Lwyd?' 'Christ,' I says, 'is that wise?' But by then Beef and Brawn were egging us on, saying, 'C'mon boys, have a bit of a laugh. Do you good."

"So we trek up to Crichton. I felt it soon as I stepped out the pub. Cold air probably. Went straight to my head. And my chest. Wheezing away, I was. But anyway, we got to the sheds out the yard there and Beef rummages behind the ploughs and the barrows and there in the far corner at the back is this horse's skull. Bloody huge, it is. Great cathedral of a thing. Gouged eye sockets, bleached bones, great big gaping jaw and teeth like piano keys. I know we've had the thing come knocking at our door in the past, but shakes me, it does."

"I took the head and the pole," says Jack, butting in, the ale's starting to talk now. "Said, 'You three can take the body, go under the bloody sheet, get hold of the pole.'"

George takes up the story again:

"So Beef goes into the farm and comes back with one of his mother's white base sheets without her knowing. Don't ask me how. Not one for late nights is Dorothy. Anyway, and he's got these ribbons and bows that he's taken from her sewing box. 'Where's the bloody bells?' he asks, bold now, loud. 'We'll have to make do without them,' says Brawn. 'Couldn't find no bells. They'll hear us coming anyhow. Make their ears ring.'"

"Off we trek," George says, in full flow, "him wedged into the skull and us three, one behind the other, the white sheet over the top of us so all you could see was four pairs of feet. Shouting, we were, top of our voices, as we plodded up towards Welsh Moor –"

"You never did?" interrupts Ellen. "You wouldn't dare."

"As I said, *his* idea," George went on. "Didn't feel mad at the time. That's the thing, isn't it? Cold, though. Freezing, we were, out there under the stars, the moon full, just the flimsy sheet on us and the alcohol coursing through our veins. And *him* leading us, blind."

"We trudged up over the common to the top of the rise and then Clever here says 'Let's break into a trot, boys. Bit of a warm up to the main event.' So there we are clip-clopping along the lane, lifting our knees high and keeping time with each other, our breath coming fast and hot under the cotton. 'Slow down,' I says, as I feel us reaching Parc- y-Rhedyn, 'we'll have no voices left.'"

"You know where we are now, sis, just coming round the bend to Prysg. 'They're still up', Jack says, 'more candles than I can count lined up along the sills in the front window'. So, I say to the boys, 'Funny how old Matthias and Daddy's Boy weren't down the pub tonight.' And Brawn says, 'The boy, most likely. Wouldn't leave the boy alone up there. Not on New Year's Eve.' And Beef says, 'Harold's not a boy though, is he?' And we all go a bit subdued after that. Sad, isn't it? Child in a man's body. Perhaps that's why that bastard is the way he is. I don't know."

"So we're in the yard then. Can feel the cobbles under my boots. Gut's going over. Excited. And scared. Wondering what sort of reaction we're going to get. Whether we'll get invited in or a bucket of water thrown over us. We didn't have to wait long. We're outside the front porch then, when Jack counts us in: One, two three... And then we're off, full voice, for the wassailing. Jack, go on by, give us a few bars, let Ellen hear that bass voice of yours."

Jack rises from the table and clears his throat theatrically. Like a music hall professional, he begins:

Once I was a young horse
And in my stable gay
I had the best of everything
Of barley oats and hay
But now I am an old horse
My courage is getting small
I'm 'bliged to eat the sour grass
That grows beneath the wall...

His voice booms through Mount Pleasant, and as he finishes, he gesticulates wildly and takes a bow.

Ellen claps her hands and shouts, "Bravo, forgotten what a fine voice you have. God forgive me for my sins, fibber that I am."

George takes up the story again, "And Jack here is inside the head and pulling a bit of baling twine and snapping the bloody horse's jaw, open, close, open, close.

"With that, old Matthias comes to the door, shouting, 'Who the hell's that?' And as the door opens, he says, 'Christ.' That's all: 'Christ.' And I could feel his shock come through the sheet. 'Well you'd better come in. Wouldn't be a Christian if I didn't invite you over the threshold, you pissed, pagan drunkards.' And I'm thinking, he's a fine one talking. But I don't say anything. Nice and safe under the sheet."

"So, in we troop and do a few more wassails. Got a hell of a thirst on me by then and am hoping he wouldn't be mean with the drink. Can feel the heat of the fire coming through the fabric, smell the wood smoke. Lovely. Better than the sweat off the three hunks stuck inside with me. I'm wondering for a minute who does the fires here without a woman in the house. Who looks after Harold, sees to his needs, or whether he's just left to get on with it."

"And?" asks Ellen, shifting forward on her chair. "Was Richard there?"

"I thought you'd never ask," says George.

"C'mon. Want to know."

"He was there. And Harold. When we took off our regalia, we could see the three of them. They'd just been sitting around the fire. Their glasses were on the little side tables. Harold was just sitting; not saying anything, of course. Just making mumbling noises and pressing his hands over his ears and then tapping his fingers on the back of his hand. Fair dos, Matthias was polite, for once. Gracious, too. Kept the rum flowing till we got warm again and our cheeks glowed with the spirits and the heat of the burning wood. Strange set-up – without a woman. Really could do with a woman there."

"Did he say anything about me: Richard, that is? Did he say we'd talked after the funeral?"

"Aye, he said you'd talked in the veg patch. Said you'd looked peaky. Hoped you were well now. Told me to wish you a very Happy New Year."

"That all?"

"Aye, that's all. Truth," butts in Jack, "straight from the horse's mouth."

"Aye, that's all. Truth," mirrors George, his laughter ending up a coughing fit.

"Very funny," says Ellen. "Very funny indeed."

"Well you did ask," says George.

The twins decide to do the bare minimum: it's a holiday, after all. The rest of the world is still sleeping or out there having fun. They tell Ellen that they'll be back in for an early lunch and then they should all go out, blow the cobwebs away before it gets dark.

"When Mother comes down, ask her if she wants to come," Jack says. "She could do with a change of scenery. Stuck in the house all the time."

"We all could," says Ellen. "Falling in around my ears."

"Well you'll be safe enough with those whoppers," says Jack.

"Get out of here. Cows'll have udders down to the ground, poor girls, if you don't milk them soon," laughs Ellen. "Be like old Eva at the post office."

"That's not very kind, Ellen. Rot in hell, you will," says George, putting on his overcoat and hat.

"Where we going, then?"

"It's still way below freezing out there," says Jack as he opens the back door. "I say Broad Pool. Be frozen solid. We'll all go skating. I'll get Mother on the ice too. Get her to laugh."

"If you can persuade her to do that, you're a better man than I am, Gunga Din," laughs George.

After they leave, Ellen goes to the dairy and takes down the brush, the mop and the old galvanised bucket, and gets cracking in the kitchen. There are major things to be sorted out soon, like the trail of debris William has left. Bills. Debts. Land. God only knows what he's got stuffed into that sloping desk. Ellen has been finding it hard to shift it from her mind, but today's not the day. Today's the day for taking control of what she can. She'll worry about the rest of her problems, later. For now, she'll sweep away the dust and the dirt that the old year's left behind, scrub the floor, mop through, wipe and polish until it's as good as she can get it. She knows she feels better when she's active, but for a brief moment she wonders if she's turning into her mother.

Chapter 13

"You won't get me onto that ice, mind," says Eleanor as the boys give her a leg up onto the bench seat of the horse and cart.

"We'll see about that," laughs Jack as he takes up the rein, Celt all brushed and spruced up, bedecked in his brasses that shine golden in the sunlight.

"All the junk in the back," says Ellen turning from the bench to smile at George sprawled out on the boards in the cart behind, flat cap on his head, blanket pulled up to his chin, and arms crossed over his chest.

He's there along with the worn leather lace-up boots and the blades and the metal tray sledges that haven't seen the light of day for years.

"Remember when Father made these trays?" Ellen asks.

They all fall silent. Ellen's in William's shed in the yard again, sitting on the work bench, her legs dangling over the edge. She likes the solidness of it, the way it bows in the middle with the weight of the years, the grooves and scratches of the chisel over time. It's just him and her in this private little hive of activity, the air thick with the scent of sap and unseasoned wood. The floor is carpeted with wood shaving and sawdust, the newly axed logs stacked neatly in the far corner, waiting to dry out, for the resin to stop running. All his tools are hanging up on the wall behind the block: polished wooden handles, shining metal, arranged in ascending order of size: hammers, chisels, fret saws, saws, hand drills, mallets, axes. There are drawers and compartments with clips and bolts and tacks and nails and screws and hinges: all the things he needed to keep things together, keep his life on track. And a spirit level.

And there's bits and pieces of flaking corrugated iron and rusty old horse shoes of all sizes tacked to the wall, open-side up for luck. Held between his gnarled hands is a sheet of old tinplate that the works at Penclawdd gave him, he says, touching the tip of his nose repeatedly with his index finger. *Don't know exactly where it came from but it'll make a damned good fast tray when I'm done with it.* So Ellen covers her ears with her palms as he takes down a hammer and starts beating around the edges, to form a narrow rim. Tap, tap, tap, tap, meticulously around the perimeter of the thing, blow by blow, beating the life out of it until it is transformed into a tray. He drills holes into the lip at the front. *There,* he says, *bit of baling twine in that and she'll go like a rocket.*

"You've had some fun out of them, mind, over the years," says Eleanor, her voice vibrating with the rhythmic jolt of the cart as it aches up the hill. "Where does the time go?"

"Remember when it snowed and we took them up the quarry? Went like hell down the sliding rock?" says George.

"And that hot day after we'd finished on the hay and we all went in the back of the cart down to Langenny? Hundred miles an hour down those dunes?" says Jack.

"Hard to remember him happy like that," says Eleanor. "But he was happy with you children. There were good times through it all. But it was never the same."

"C'mon now, Mother. Let's make the most of today," says Ellen as Jack reaches the crossroads at the top of the village. "We'll have enough to contend with in the next few weeks."

They turn left into the sun. Its rays are weak, but offer the gentlest hint of warmth on their upturned faces. They rumble past Crichton Farm on the right where all is quiet today; the men inside probably sleeping it off. On past Cil Ifor tops on the left, and on past the fork in the track that snakes up onto Welsh Moor. Ellen turns back to look, watching the farm fade into the distance; but she doesn't say anything. Eleanor gives Ellen one of her looks and shrugs her shoulders; Ellen doesn't have to reply.

Celt labours on, the cart weighed down with its heavy load.

"Wonder if Celt is missing him?" asks Eleanor.

"He won't show anything, either, Mother," comes George's voice from the rear. "Just plods on day by day. All any of us can do, really, I suppose."

The depleted family trundles on, past the dark wooded lane on the right that leads to the big house at Cae Forgan. On until they round the final bend before they are confronted by vast open skies above the expanse of Cefn Bryn which rises in front of them like a beast with a broad brown back.

"Looks lovely," sighs Ellen. "Always felt I could breathe, here. Hard to think it's only a step from the village. So different. Unfenced. Free. Another world."

"And quiet today without all that racket coming from the saw mills," says Eleanor as they approach the small junction onto the Bryn.

No hiss of steam comes from Cilibion. No see-saw rhythm of saws. No shouts of men. Only the sight of newly felled trees stacked at one end of the yard and, piled at the other, pale fence posts not yet weathered by time and the elements.

"Funny with that steam engine off," says George. "Like the heart of the place has stopped beating."

"You've got a lovely way with words, George," says Eleanor. "Like a poet, you are."

"Won't get him anywhere, words," says Jack, "but I'll give him that. He's got a lovely turn of phrase."

They take a right onto the Red Road, as the twins call it: hardly a road at all but a dusty red track formed from the same old red sandstone that formed the Bryn. It feels old as time itself here. The track bisects the Bryn: the flank rising steeply on their left, separating the wild and untamed north of the peninsula from the softer, perhaps more pasteurised, south. Broad Pool glistening within feet of the track on their right.

Ellen peers into the crowds that have flocked to the ice, their fast-moving silhouettes indistinguishable at this distance against the blue backdrop of afternoon light; while other dark shapes lace the edges.

"Don't know why, but I thought we'd have it to ourselves," says Ellen.

"You must be kidding. Everybody's got the same idea when it freezes over like this," says Jack.

"Suppose so," says Ellen. "Have to make the best of it."

Jack pulls up Celt onto the spiky frozen grass on the left, opposite the iced-over pool.

"Never seen so many carts here," says George.

Ellen's eyes dart across the tethered shires and the empty carts, looking for any she might recognise.

"Looking for anyone special?" asks Jack.

"No. Why?" asks Ellen.

"Just wondering, that's all," laughs Jack. "Will he be here or won't he? That's the question."

"Be quiet, will you. Not interested. Not. At. All. Full stop."

The boys help Eleanor down. She's fussing now about the fact that she's still in black, that she shouldn't be out enjoying herself, that it's too soon. Inappropriate. What will all these people think of her?

"I don't care a hoot, what they think of me," says Ellen. "And you shouldn't, either. You did all you could, Mother. Couldn't save Father from himself."

"D'you think so?"

"I know so. He'll be looking down and wanting to see a smile on your face. Hold your head up. To hell with them all."

The boys and Ellen get into their skates and lace the parched boots up tightly. Eleanor stands in amongst the crowds of people around the pool and watches as they take to the ice.

"I'll look after the trays," she says. "Have a bit of a chat."

After a couple of tentative steps, Ellen is ready. It's something you don't forget, like riding a horse or a cycle. The memory is lodged in her muscles. And anyway, she's had the chance to skate more often since she left. Winters in Hoboken were more defined than they were here. They came earlier. Bit harder. Lasted longer. A frozen lake was the norm. This was just a tiny frozen pool, for goodness' sake. For a moment, she thinks of Hoboken and how the sheer throb of it had taken her breath away when she'd seen it for the first time. She's been a city girl for the last two years; got used to the scale of the buildings stretching endlessly into the sky, the crowds of people jostling for space in the streets, the melding of different tongues she'd never heard before. People like her searching for something new. Or perhaps escaping the old. But then the image melts away as quickly as it appeared. Where does she belong?

She places her arms to her sides, tucks them into her body and leans forward. She pushes hard on those big, strong thighs of hers, feels them gird her into motion. Push to the left, glide; push to the right, glide; setting up her peculiar rhythm, getting into the flow. Left skate, right skate, left skate, right skate, metal blades grazing the surface, narrow groves marking out her passage. She loves the sound of the scratches she is carving into the ice. Abrasive. Grating. Faster and faster, she skims across the ice, each glide longer than the one before, leaning into the turns as she rounds the far edge of this frozen and transient playground. She knows she's not graceful. God knows she'd never have made a ballerina. But here she's powerful. Strong as any of the men – even her brothers – who are straining to keep up with her. She's got stamina, too. Built to last. On and on she could go, surging forward without fear.

Her momentum makes the still air stir, as she attacks it headlong. Its cold gnaws at her cheeks, which glow with exertion. The thought of the blood running into them makes her feel good. Wholesome. She'd like Richard to see her like this, ruddy and wild. Like Richard to inhale the scent of her. She can smell it herself, her own woman smell; the musky sweat making damp circles under her armpits, beneath the tightness of her encaged breasts, along the elastic of her knickers.

Richard. Richard. His name is repeating in her head, he's lodged under her skin, running in her blood that is boiling over with the exercise and with something other, too? Perhaps the melding of everything it was possible to feel for one man. All she knows is that he has the capacity to do things to her. And cruelty. He proved it. Discarded her like chaff on the wind. A barren husk. He was a risk she could never take again. Yet, his eyes come into her head, those blue, navy-rimmed irises. His forearms; beautifully strong limbs. Even the smell of him. Of rain on his pullover, the distinctive sweat of his labour. It won't go away even though she's free as a bird in flight and she's skating, skating, skating on ice. She can't help wondering. Without the physical distance of the Atlantic, his presence is crystalising in the cold January air. It seems two years is not nearly enough to erase memories so deeply lodged.

As she weaves through the capes and the coats and the mufflers and the hats, she's wondering. Is it him? Let it be him. Let it not be him. But what then? She clears him from her imaginings, won't allow him to cloud her pathway, stand in her way. She darts through the children clinging to the pool's edge, cuts through the young lads who think they're good. She senses them turn and admire her as she flies through, realising that they're not as good as her. Never will be.

She breathes hard and fast. Forcibly. Every out-breath a sign that she is here. In the moment. Just being without thought and intellect, just the joy of her own young and fit body. Her heart is pulsing too fast, beating out the message that she is very much alive. Hypnotised by the motion of her own body, she circles the perimeter. She is moving independently of her mind, of her own free will. If she were to keep going and keep increasing the effort, the pace, the speed, she would surely leave the ground behind her, surge into the air, and who knows where that might take her.

She wants to take the pin out of her hat, hurl it across the ice, unclip her hair. What might it be like to have it loose and trailing out behind her, free-flowing in her wake as she whizzes on the solid ice beneath her blades? She hears the swish of her dress as it skims the surface. How she'd love to shed those acres of fabric, trade them in for one pair of trousers. Then she wouldn't be impeded. Then nothing would get in her way.

She feels reckless. There's something about the fact that neither this state of being nor the frozen water beneath her will last. She has to make the most of it, before the cracks and splits appear.

Eleanor waves at her as she passes. A wave that says, *Be careful.* A wave that says, *I'm here. I need you. Don't leave me.* Her mother's face looks distorted as she speeds past. Twisted by Ellen's angle of vision and the years of worry and caring that ended only in death. It's bleached out. Devoid of the lust for life. It makes Ellen feel a touch of hopelessness. All the futility of life's struggle in one fleeting glimpse. She fears it might be infectious.

The twins smile at her as she passes. Smiles that say, *It's good having you home, sis. We need you. Don't leave us. Not with all the mess we've got to contend with.* Smiles that tug at her, that have pulled like invisible threads over the ocean that has divided them across the last couple of years. They would always do the same. Tug at her insides, as would Richard, damn him!

Her mother's little black-gloved wave is the signal that it is time to slow down. She's been standing there too long on her own. Ellen's going to get her on that tray, while there is still time. She skates up to her and beckons the boys.

"Right, your turn now, Mother," she gasps, "I've had enough."

"No arguing. On you get," says Jack, spreading some old sacking onto the tray.

George takes his mother by the arm as she places one timid foot in front of the other onto the ice.

"I'm going to fall," she shouts. "Don't let me go."

"I've got you. We're all here," he says. "Just ease yourself down slowly."

"I feel silly," she says slowly and quietly, "old and silly."

Ellen and the boys smooth the sacking for their mother to sit on, not letting go of her until she's settled on the tray. Ellen is touched by the expression of warmth on her mother's face in response to their tenderness. It's a rare sight to see her like this, her troubles momentarily easing, along with the tightness of her lips. Tears begin to spill down her mother's ruddied cheeks.

"Are you crying, Mother?" asks Jack as he sees Eleanor wipe her eyes.

"Good gracious, no. It's the cold. Always makes my eyes play up. It'll happen to you when you're my age."

Ellen unlaces her skates and puts her boots back on. She takes the space her mother has vacated at the edge of the pool. She watches as Jack and George tie the baling twine that is attached to the tray around their girths so that they end up looking like a pair of pit ponies. She sees her father again in the shed. Hears his words: *She'll go like a rocket*. Eleanor grips the metal rims on either side of her, hanging on for grim death, as Jack and George skate away in perfect synchrony.

The sight of her mother's black hat and her broad, black-coated back, her bottom spread across the tin sledge, is quite ridiculous, making Ellen laugh. She watches as her mother skims the ice at speed, and looks forward to seeing her expression by the time she rounds the curve at the far end and skids back towards Ellen. When her mother is indeed hurtling towards her, there is a look on her face that she hasn't seen since she was a child. It makes her fill up. She would like to remember her mother as she is this minute. Always.

The time is passing too quickly, the light fading. Shadows are falling across the mottled heathland, draining the colour from the sparse grass and bog rushes. Ponies are swishing their tails and turning away from the pool, sensing that the day is ending. There is an agitation in the air that comes with dusk: murmurs of starlings create strange black shapes overhead and then they are gone. Wild grey geese make their characteristic honking and then fall into silence.

Ellen looks north across the estuary. Low cumulus clouds are banking far out on the horizon. They're in for a change.

Chapter 14

"Did it always used to rain as much as this? Does it ever get light? You know, *really* light?" asks Ellen as she stands in the kitchen looking out over the estuary.

"Worse things in life than weather, maid," says Elizabeth from her perch in the corner.

"Doesn't feel like. Not at the minute. Can't tell where the sea ends and the sky begins. Everything's smudged together. Or rubbed out. Was it always this grey in Gower?"

She uses her fingers to list all the tones of grey, chanting them out loud to anyone who cares to listen: "Limestone grey, wood-pigeon grey, Llanelli grey, estuary grey, even the grass is grey – where has all the colour gone?"

"You've got 'em this morning," says Eleanor, encased in her apron at the range, polishing the hob covers.

"Just hate January. The emptiness of it all," sighs Ellen.

"You need to get out. Walk it off," says Eleanor.

"In this?" she says, gesturing at the window.

"Wrap up and you'll be fine. For once I agree with her in the corner there: worse things than weather. All you need is the right clothes."

"Just for once, Mother, you might be right. Need to get out of this room before it buries me alive... Sorry!"

"Talking of which, we need to have a get-together. All of us. Once the boys are finished outside and washed up. See what sort of a mess he's left."

"Right. Then I'll make the best of what light there is."

With her long oilskin coat almost reaching her ankles and her brimmed hat pulled tight down over her brow, Ellen sets off purposefully in her stout walking brogues. Every step is a reconnection with the past.

Only now, for the first time since she's back, may she touch the whipping stones standing proud on the village green. How she'd kept on seeing them in her mind's eye when she was in America! They seemed a symbol of everything she turned her back on: childhood, family, the known. But they also signalled a deeper association with the past: the generations before hers: those who farmed this place, carved out a living, made a future for their children. One that she'd denied herself. For what? Because she wanted to be somewhere she didn't have to be poor just because she was a girl? Where she could aspire to be what she wanted? Was it, rather, that she was not so much running towards something, as running away from a place where duty and inheritance weighed heavier than any future she might craft herself? Today in the mist, it's all a jumble.

She runs the flat of her palm across the raised pock-marked limestone of the megalith on the upper green. It is solid. Impregnated with the touch of a thousand other hands. Hands that sweated together to move and hoist this stone into place from the lower green. Why, she does not know. They must have had their reasons. She's heard stories that they were paid in pints of ale for their labour at the Welcome to Town. She touches the weathered small hoops of iron, two on the flat face of the stone towards the top, two towards the bottom. The brown-red flakes of rust are damp and fragile. She rubs her palms together to try and free herself of it, but it clings. It's not easy to shake yourself free of the past.

She remembers her father's stories. Always the stories. The one about this standing stone being here for those that didn't keep to the path of righteousness. It must have been when he still kept the faith. Believed in a God who knew right from wrong. There were tales of those who were tethered, hands to the top rings, feet to the bottom, and were left there on show to the villagers to do to them as they would: *that would sort 'em*, he'd say. There's a few she'd like to tie to this stone now. Give them a good thrashing. Perhaps that's why she and the twins had called them the whipping stones when they were young? Who knows what's fact and what's fiction?

She looks down at the village: the old woollen mill at Stavel Hagar is disappearing. Stone by stone, it's being dismantled. Soon all that remains will be a heap of Gower rubble where once there was life. Everything in Gower is grey and crumbling or turning to rust. She wonders what will take its place in the future. Realises that nothing lasts forever. One minute the looms were rattling and the women weaving and the blankets being spread on beds and the backs of chairs and snuggling poorly children, and the next, nothing.

But the flour mill's still going, the grain being stacked in the eaves of Stanley's mill on the pond, the grain being ground, the flour being milled, the people being fed. For the time being.

And next to the mill, there's Bay Tree Cottage with its ancient dry stone walls, yellowed with lichen, and its one acre of pear and apple orchards. She wonders if the trunks of those trees hold the laughter of her childhood and girlhood. Her and Emily Dix, swinging off the boughs on fraying ropes, undaunted by the twine burning their hands. Those two were made of strong stuff, it turned out. Stuff that would see them both living on the other side of the world, carving out their own destinies, free of expectations. And the Butter Pool, as it was called, there in the garden. It was also known in the village as the holy well. Up from it came cool spring water. Some said it could make you fertile. *Didn't work for me, though,* thinks Ellen. *Not when it was needed.*

She thinks again of Emily. Little Emily, now grown-up. Lovely Emily of the letters, who graduated from college in New York. If it hadn't been for the Dix family's leaving for America a couple of years before Ellen, and her correspondence with Emily, she would never have gone. At least not as quickly as she did, even though it was with a heavy heart.

She misses Emily and her chats. She'll miss her even more when Emily uproots from Hoboken to take up her position in the elementary school in Rutherford, New Jersey. Mr. and Mrs. Dix have already settled there. Too good an opportunity for a clever engineer like Tom Dix to miss: Rutherford with its proud new iron bridge over the Passaic and its wonderful new glass railways station, its wide avenues and green spaces.

She can see Emily there in her element in the leafy suburbs. Can see her there with a husband and some children one day.

Could she see herself there, too? Everything seems possible on the other side of the ocean. She could work hard, make her way in the world, breathe the air in those leafy suburbs. Perhaps she could be a teacher if she wanted to enough? Perhaps she could have the husband and the children as well? Just like Emily. And then Richard slips in unasked, fitting seamlessly into the picture frame. It isn't impossible that he'd leave the farm – if there was a strong enough tug to pull him away? Farmers can turn their hands to anything. Richard can build and fix anything with a mallet and a spanner and his good brain. He sees what needs to be done. Brings it about. He could easily learn a new trade, become an engineer with Mr. Dix. He could build those new bridges and those new glass railway stations. He could become the person he is capable of being.

Yes, she will miss Emily and the life she breathed into her, the oxygen that fuelled the little spark of hope that remained in the dark ashes of disappointment. She thinks about that tattered paper secreted in that book on her bedroom shelf, the words etched into her heart over all this time:

Your pure and thoughtful words
Speak like changeless seasons

Huh! Changeless seasons? That's a joke. But she had *actually* written it. Let her emotions pour from her heart to her head to her pen to the page. Like blood-letting. And now here is Richard again sloping into the dark recesses of her mind. His scent. Now here is the possibility of a future – if he were allowed it. Right here where there are all those hues of grey. Where life is no longer simply black and white.

Chapter 15

After lunch, Eleanor empties William's desk of all its contents. In readiness for the family meeting, stacks of yellowing paper, inked in William's faltering hand, are carried to the kitchen table. There is a hole in each paper from the metal spike kept on the desk. William's pending spike.

"No more 'pending'. Get this sorted out once and for all," she says to Elizabeth. "A good clear out is what we need. Will you be joining us, Mother?"

"No, I'll stay out of it here on the settle, if that's all right with you, maid? Leave it to the youngsters. The able minded and the able bodied. Can't stand all that thinking and remembering. Not at my age."

"Please yourself, then. But don't say you weren't asked."

The twins have washed and shaved and put on clean shirts in the middle of a working day, sensing the enormity of the occasion. Ellen has changed into a dress, plain and dark. Eleanor has even taken off her pinny, draped it across the rail of the range ready to put on again later, however long that might be.

"Right," she says, sinking her body into a chair at the side of the table. "Ready when you are."

Apart from the scraping of the chair-legs as the twins and Ellen join their mother at the table, there isn't a word. Just the tick of the clock.

"You can all chip in. Don't know much about business, me. Only about work. Or the legalities and the practicalities of what's to be done. Leave that to you with the brains. Never had an education, me," says Eleanor.

"Might not be that bad, Mother," says George, "we'll get there somehow. Manage if we all pull together."

Ellen watches her mother's face. She hasn't had much of an education herself, either. Left school at fourteen but at least she can read and write, and she carried on learning from books of her own volition, just like George. She wonders why it isn't in Jack's blood to bother. But then again, he has more immediate things to worry about. Ellen can only imagine what it must feel like to be her mother, there on the fringes, the ground falling in around her, without the other-worldliness of books to lose herself in, if only for a while.

"Forty acres is what we've got. That is fact. It's what Mount Pleasant is," says Jack without sentiment. "That's the reality."

"Can't believe it's all gone; that he'd do that to me, to us," says Eleanor twisting her handkerchief.

"Wasn't father who did it to us," interjects Ellen, "it was the illness. He couldn't help it."

"Illness? Illness?" shouts Eleanor. "Don't know where you get these notions from, my girl. It was the drink. Pure and simple. And those cronies he chose to spend his time with. Evil. The lot of it. Illness, indeed."

"Look," says George, ever the diplomat, "Ellen might be right. Don't know about illness but he couldn't seem to help himself and this is the result. Where we are now. Forty acres. And five adults to support. Not pretty, is it?"

"Impossible," says Ellen. "Things will have to change."

"Don't like change," says Eleanor. "Had more than enough change, already."

"Not all change is bad, Mother," says George breathily, the faintest gasps from his chest audible in the still and charged room.

"Well, we can't change the past," says Ellen. "I know that more than most. Let's see what we can salvage."

She sweeps the mound of papers towards her, and wades through them while the others sit waiting.

"Well?" says Eleanor.

"Seems he's settled all he's owed in the gambling. The top fields at Welsh Moor signed over to Jeremiah Grove, so no I.O.Us there. Pastures at Crichton and Llethryd signed over to the Beynons. We knew about that so nothing to shock so far. No secrets here, I don't think. Poor old soul, he tried to keep everything tidy, fair play."

"And the Croft? Those six acres I loved? What about that? That's the last thing he blew away on a whim. The shake of a dice. A tot of rum. Our future," sobs Eleanor.

"Calm down, Mother," says Jack. "Give Ellen a chance. I don't think that was finalised, from what I remember."

"He's right, Mother. There's still an I.O.U. on that. Still pending," says Ellen.

"Who's he owing, Ellen?" asks George.

"You'll never guess," says Ellen.

"Who?" asks Jack.

"For goodness' sake, maid, spit it out. Haven't got all day," comes the voice from the settle in the corner.

"Matthias Tucker. Prysg Farm," says Ellen. "Bloody Matthias Tucker, of all the people."

"Language, Ellen, please," says Eleanor.

"For goodness' sake, Mother," says Ellen, "stick to the point."

"Did you know, Mother?" asks Jack.

"Not exactly know. An inkling, maybe. He didn't actually say who he'd lost it to. And then I couldn't say, could I? Only have made things worse with Ellen home and everything."

"So it's not official then?" says George. "Not yet. Even Matthias is perhaps doing the decent thing – if there is a decent thing in all this – to act with decorum, to not come banging at our door for payment, for what's rightfully his now, until the right length of time passes after Father's death."

"He'll not have his pickings," says Ellen determinedly. "Over my dead body he'll have the Croft. Leave it with me."

"That's my girl," shouts Elizabeth from the sidelines, raising her stick in the air.

"Calm down, Gran. Think of your heart," says George.

"Don't much care about my heart, anymore. Just you lot, now."

"What are you going to do, Ellen? Don't want any more falling out, any more upset. My nerves can't take it. Enough on my plate. Don't want any more shame on this family, either," says Eleanor.

"Shame? I've got nothing to be ashamed of. Is that what I brought you? Shame? Because I couldn't be married off? Wasn't any use?" shouts Ellen.

"Look, everybody, let's not create a scene here," says George.

"I said, leave it to me. You'll have that land back. Final," says Ellen. And she bangs her fist on the wooden table, the vibrations making the legs shake.

"I'll make a pot of tea," says Eleanor getting up and reaching for the armour of her pinny. "Settle us all down."

She places the kettle on the hob and wills it to come to the boil. At the table the conversation continues, George trying to keep things on an even keel.

"I've been thinking," says George.

"Always a dangerous thing," laughs Jack.

"Listen. I'm serious. You don't have to be that good at arithmetic to know that the sums don't add up here at the moment. Forty acres. Two men. Three women. And that's without Annie coming here goodness knows when. If I go, get a job, get digs somewhere nearby, it means that the land goes further. Like the loaves and fishes. And I can get to contribute a bit to Mother in the meantime. And it means that you won't have to wait to marry Annie. You've been waiting long enough and the poor girl is desperate for you. You're the head of the house now, Jack. Can't have two heads. The chair's not big enough for both of us. Look."

And they all look at William's vacant carver still empty at the top of the table.

"Your arithmetic's not that good, George," says Ellen tersely.

"Sorry?" says George.

"Division. Ever stopped to think that there are three possible heads? That the chair can't accommodate three of us?"

"What? You?" asks Jack with a smile.

"Yes, me. Why not? I'm the eldest. And the one with a good head on my shoulders," says Ellen.

"But, you're a woman," shouts Eleanor across the kitchen.

"Why 'but'?" says Ellen. "Why not 'and'?"

"It's just..." says Eleanor.

"It's just –. It's just –. It's not 'just': that's the truth. What the hell d'you think you've been doing for almost thirty years, Mother? I mean Father was no great shakes was he?"

"She's got a point, mind," says Elizabeth. "Even though he was my son, he didn't have much of a head for business. I'll give her that."

"Exactly," says Ellen.

"For goodness' sake, Ellen. Get your feet on the ground, Don't know what's in that head of your sometimes," says Eleanor.

Ellen feels an overwhelming anger and sense of injustice that she can't be bothered to go on trying to articulate. There are no allies in the room, apart from Elizabeth in the corner and she doesn't want to make it difficult for her. After all, Elizabeth will still be sitting on the settle, living with the consequences of the ripples Ellen's creating in the house, long after she herself will have upped and left. She often wonders why it seems she has always found it easier to get on with her grandmother than her mother, that the real bond seems to have skipped a generation. Is that how it works with women?

"Come on then, George. Let's hear what the boys have to say," says Ellen.

"Yes, what are you thinking?" asks Jack. "You won't go far, will you? Couldn't bear that."

"No, not far. But we're not joined at the hip. New Lynch. They're expanding all the time and pushing out drift mines under the estuary. They're crying out for men," explains George.

"But your chest?" shouts Eleanor from the range. "I can't have you going there with that chest of yours."

"Dust's no different from seed, Mother. All the same. Don't worry. They're paying a good few shillings a week, and Mrs. Tanner up at Malt Hall has rooms, been looking for lodgers since her husband went. Could all work out well for everybody," says George.

"It could work for you too, Jack, the coal," says Ellen. She's going to make sure she says her piece. That they can see she's got a brain.

"What d'you mean? Farmer I am, not a collier!"

"No, not underground. Haulage. You need to expand what you do. Go into new and different things. Get additional income."

"Move coal from A to B in the cart?" asks Jack.

"Yes, and other things too. Produce from the local farms back and fore to Swansea Market on a Saturday. And then there's rush out the marsh and other farmers' hay. And the lime. When I was out walking today I noticed how much was going on at the quarry at the top of the hill. No doubt they'd be interested in you. Put it to them. You could build a nice little business for you and little Annie here. I can see the future: J.I. Thomas and Sons. Farmers and Hauliers. Who knows? Though I think E.E. Thomas and Daughters has a nice ring about it too, don't you?"

No one rises to the bait. There is just a silence that lasts a little longer than the normal turn-taking in conversation.

"Well that's all sorted, then," shouts Elizabeth. "A cup of tea is in order."

"Just you now, Ellen," says Eleanor as she puts the freshly brewed pot in front of her. "What about you?"

Ellen doesn't answer. There's nothing to say. She pours her brothers a cup of tea each and then one for herself. She brings the cup up slowly to her lips, blows on the weak, barely-brown liquid, and allows herself to get momentarily lost in the fug.

Chapter 16

George tries not to disturb Jack as he extracts himself from the bed. It's not easy with the weight of the sheets, blankets and eiderdown, not to mention the outdoor coats they've had to place on top overnight. Even though their body heat is normally enough, these early February nights have been bitter.

It's not yet light at 4.30am, the other residents of Mount Pleasant are still all tucked up and snug; but George has a three mile walk to New Lynch ahead of him this morning. Shift starts at 6.00am. Can't be late on his first day. Though he can't see Jack, he can hear him deep in sleep: the long easy breaths, no hint of a rattle. It'll be a momentous day for him too, left alone on the farm, when he rises at first light. George fills up at the thought of being separated.

Even through his knitted socks, the floor is cold on his feet as he pads across the bedroom in his long-johns. He creaks open the door and treads quietly along the landing, down the stairs and into the kitchen. The warmth from the range is a comfort, as is the flicker of the candle he lights. On the table is a tea cloth. He unfolds it to see inside what his mother has packed him for the day. It's a lunch of sorts: a hunk of bread and dripping, a slice of cheese, the smallest piece of teisen lap, the currants few. Twelve hours is a long time on a growling stomach. But they have to eke out what they have now. He wraps the contents back in the tea towel and places it in his little canvas work bag. He brings the kettle to the boil and makes a can of tea and places that in the bag too. He's not hungry now. Anticipation, probably. Suddenly he feels like a little boy again on his first day at school. As he stands at the range, he touches his mother's pinny hanging over the rail, wants to cling for a little while longer to its white strings.

He stands in his long-johns on the mat in front of the range. The cat is purring at his feet, rubbing its neck and fur against his calves in a soothing, monotonous way. It's going to be hard to leave this kitchen.

He needs to get dressed. He's a worker underground, now. The less he puts on, the less he'll have to take off. They've said there's no need for a shirt. But he puts his flannel waistcoat on over his singlet and ties his checked muffler to cover his neck and the covered buttons at the top of the vest. He'll look grown up and respectable like the men he's seen walking back and fore to the mines. He steps into his britches and buttons them up, takes down his jacket, decides to leave it open. Finally, he puts on his flat peaked cap, tugs it down and considers whether he'll wear it at an angle. It presses on the tops of his ears, forcing them to stick out even more under the band of the cap.

He must look a sight. But this is his new uniform. This is what he'll show to the world. This is what he is now. Not a farmer. A collier. He sits on his father's worn old winged chair at the side of the range and bends to lace his cracked leather boots. What would his father make of him now? He hopes he'd be proud. That he wouldn't be seen as selfish.

He stretches out his hands in front of him. A vain habit he has. He splays his fingers, then clenches his fists, back and fore, back and fore as he sometimes does with the tendons of chicken claws. They're his father's hands. Wonders how they'll fare underground. He's always been proud of his hands. And his nails. Kept them scrubbed and cut short, cuticles trimmed. And when he's finished, he slings his bag over his shoulder, unlocks the kitchen door and walks out into the morning, leaving Mount Pleasant dressed as a real man.

He stops at the lavatory in the yard. His bladder and his bowels are in turmoil. Yet everything around is still and calm. The stars are blue-bright and the moon, full and frosty suspended over the estuary. It casts a magical pathway of light on the surface of the water, so white he feels it has substance, that he could walk across it to the other side to who knows where.

But his lead toe-capped boots are keeping him on this side of the Loughor: the side he knows. His boots are walking him towards Crofty and he wonders if the man in the moon will smile down at him from now on.

There's not a soul on the track until Common Farm, where he sees the glow of a cigarette tip coming out of the gate. It's Wilfred Jones' boy, Emlyn, and even though he can only be thirteen, if that, he's drawing on the cigarette through his young lips. No hands.

"Morning, George," he mumbles without taking the cigarette from his mouth "First day, eh?

"Aye."

"Don't worry. I'll show you the ropes."

They fall into step as they walk on together. Out of the garden gate at Brynfield emerges Hywel the Bryn. George can hear him clearing his throat before he sees him, hear the sound of phlegm hitting the dirt. Doesn't sound promising for someone with a chest like his.

"Morning, George," he says, "first day, eh? Stick with me, don't let Emlyn here lead you into any bad ways. Isn't that right, Emlyn?"

Emlyn smiles. Says nothing. George feels his own father walking in tandem with him on the track. It must be the sight of Hywel, with his white hair and white pointy beard that has conjured him up. The very age of him. Methusulah comes to mind. He's surely too old for all this.

Man by man, boy by boy, others join them as they tramp along, their bootfall sounding like soldiers marching in step towards the mine. Old men, middle-aged men, young men, youths, children; it's difficult to tell people's age in the dark when they're all dressed the same. But out of Wernhalog comes the bark of a dog, and George knows, before he sees, it will be Haydn Jones. He has a cross-terrier in his arms, as white and straggly as his owner's facial hair. It shocks him. He hadn't expected that dogs would be going down the mines.

The rhythm of their steps is hypnotic. George feels a certain comfort in that he's part of this group now. A man on his own for the first time yet very much part of something.

And there are more men joining, minute by minute. From the row of terraced houses built especially for the new mining men in Wernffrwd, come another two to join the band of workers. And they pour out from the Wern and the Rhallt, chattering in Welsh, the language of the peninsula's industrial north, not quite alien, but unintelligible apart from the odd word to his English-speaking ear. The men's feet carry them along, left, right, left, right until they round the bend at Llanmorlais, where George sees the iron viaduct and the brick and stone workings at New Lynch.

When the men assemble in the siding he sees that some of them are surely both too old and too young to be in the mines. Many have silver beards and bushy, grey moustaches that slope down sadly over their upper lips. All the men except Emlyn and he have moustaches of varying colours, shading from dark to light. George strokes his chin with his right hand, runs his finger across the top of his lips. Vows he'll not be clean-shaven for a day longer than he can help. Emlyn will have to wait that little bit longer, poor sod. George places his thumbs in his waistcoat pockets and puffs out his crackling chest. He listens to the rumble of the tram loaded with anthracite behind him. It's been a long day already and at ten to six, it hasn't yet begun.

Back at the farm, the day has started. Jack is already up and in the milking sheds, his stomach will be calling for breakfast soon.

He sits on the three-legged milking stool his father had made him in the wood shed. He'd fashioned three of them, all exactly the same, out of an old yew that had been uprooted in the churchyard the night of a great storm. *Lovely piece of wood, this*, he'd said. *Beautiful grain. Love an old bit of yew.* At the side of the stalls, the other two stools are empty now. Jack wonders how George's morning is going so far. He misses him already. Can't believe his brother is doing this for him.

The distinctive sweet smell of the cows is thick in the air: a pungent early-morning mix of warm milk and cattle-breath, the heat of the hides, the dung and ammonia in the hay. It'll take twice as long this morning without George. He feels a lesser half of a whole. The sum of their parts seemed always greater than their individual selves. "The twins –" this. "The twins –" that. When they were younger they'd tried to earn a few shillings at the quarry, only to be asked by the owner if he could have the two of them work for one wage.

He tugs on the pink teats of the swollen udders of cow number five. Another seven to go, though there's pleasure in the tough rhythmic pulling of his hands drawing down the milk, the release of the liquid into the pail wedged between his knees. The moon is still up, its light comes through the open section of the Dutch-barn door, bathing the floor at his feet in milkiness to match the contents of his pail. He hopes the moon and the stars will continue to shine down on him from now on.

He's absorbed in the sight of his own hands as he milks: strong, big-knuckled hands. Even the fingers have a strength of their own. And they're his father's hands there in the lonely dawn. And George's too, though George is more particular about his. Vain bugger. Couldn't care less, himself. Long as they're clean. He remembers that their finger prints are distinct, though, will leave different imprints on life.

The solitary low of the Jersey in the next stall breaks his thoughts. He rises and places the almost-full pail next to the door, taking care not to spill a drop. He picks up his stool and moves along, positions a fresh pail under the udders and gets into rhythm again. After a few tugs, the milk starts to flow. He likes the patterns of his life: the repetitive and familiar daily grind, the ongoing beat and predictability of the changing seasons. It's part of who he is, in the blood. He doesn't think he'd ever be able to do for George what George is doing for him.

"Bye, girls," he says to the cows as he leaves. "Take you down the bottom fields later for a bit of an airing. Starving, I am."

He carries the pails to the dairy, ready for the women to deal with later. He can smell bacon frying as he crosses the yard. *Perfect timing*, he thinks. There's a crack of light in the sky and he suddenly feels guilty about the dawn he's witnessing that George is not. George, who's an hour and a half into his first shift now, George who will be stooping in the tunnels that have been cut beneath the estuary. Even though they're not deep and no winding gear is needed in these drift mines, they're dark and constricted. He wonders how his chest is holding up. How his back is doing. Even though he's strong from physical labour, the mines are different. He'll use a new group of muscles with the pick, muscles which will groan from the crouching on his haunches and slithering on his belly to hack at the seams of anthracite. Jack can't contemplate this dirty sort of body-ache; it's not wholesome like farm work. It's a hell he could never endure. That black dust in the nostrils. That sooty taste on the tongue. Water oozing through the mud. He sees that fine torso of George's ingrained with coal, the palms of his hands black. He'll hate it getting under those nails. Jack wonders if even George's shape will change from the unfamiliar labour. Whether he'll morph into something other than his identical twin. Whether he'll resemble him at all in the end.

Here above ground, it looks like it's promising to break into a fine day. A day that George won't see, stuck beneath the estuary with just the glow of a lamp. He wonders what number will be etched on his little metal tag. All this. For him. For the farm. Is it all worth it, really? His body is aching already for his brother. He unlaces his boots and leaves them outside the kitchen door, ready to put back on when he's had his breakfast. All of a sudden he has no appetite for it, none at all.

Chapter 17

Everything and everyone at Mount Pleasant is in a state of flux after George goes underground. Only the cream has settled during the morning, rising to the top of the fresh milk in the earthenware setting dishes in the cool of the dairy. Eleanor lined them up in readiness for Jack when he finished milking, and he poured the warm contents of his pails, taking care not to spill. He wouldn't dare.

"You've still got the knack, my girl," says Eleanor later as Ellen is separating the cream from the milk with a wooden scummer and placing it into the churn. "Careful, though. Can't afford to waste."

Ellen ignores her mother and continues with the painstaking process, Eleanor standing at her shoulder, waiting for something to go wrong, something to dispute with her daughter.

"Don't like butter too ripe, myself. What about you?"

"Ripe? No chance of that in this weather. Look. My hands are blue. Not hanging around in here longer than I have to."

"You've always been such an impatient child, you know."

"Is there anything I do right, Mother?"

"Just get on with it. Don't spend your energy back-biting.

Keep your strength up for the churning. Make sure you do it right. Can sell the surplus. Want to get a good batch out of this lot before dark. Before George comes home."

"Wonder how he's getting on?" says Ellen.

"Don't want to think about it. As long as he's safe, that's all. Let's keep busy."

Ellen loves the feel of the smooth scummer in her hands. Her father had made it especially for Eleanor. Invented it, he'd said. Taken the shape of a saucer as a template and then carved it out of a bit of old oak. Natural resins would keep the germs away. Better than water. A person's stomach couldn't be too careful with milk. He drilled holes, tens of them, into the surface, like a miniature colander so that the cream could be skimmed off and the watery liquid pass through.

"Do you miss him, Mother?" asks Ellen.

"He's only been gone half a day," replies Eleanor.

"Not George, Father."

"What made you ask that now, all of a sudden?"

"Just these –, the things he left behind. Full of memories."

"Course I miss him. Not a day goes by I don't think about him," she says, picking up the pair of butter pats and stroking the grooves and ridges on the undersides. "Don't miss the worry, though. Not if I'm honest. Made these too, you know. And this churn, out of an old barrel. And this stamp here."

Ellen puts down the scummer for a minute and picks up the round butter stamp. It's worn, and the wood almost white with wear. She holds the little handle and turns the stamp upside down to look at the distinctive pattern of the four-leafed clover that William had delicately chiselled into its surface.

"Didn't bring us our fortune though, did it?" says Eleanor flatly.

"No. But his heart was in the right place."

"Suppose so. Enough, now. Costing us time, idle chit-chat."

Heads down, hopes up, the women crack on, Ellen earnestly scumming and pouring until every last dollop of cream is skimmed off into the churn, with Eleanor overseeing operations like a drill sergeant major.

Ellen begins to crank the lever. It's not heavy for her, but long and monotonous. Over and over she turns it until the sound inside the barrel changes from solid to slosh as the buttermilk drains away from the cream, which is slowly, so slowly, turning into butter, unseen, there in the dark. A little like the thoughts she has in her head: of Richard, out of sight of her mother's prying eyes and questions.

"You can do the buttermilk – ladle it into the jugs. Be lovely mashed into some spuds for supper, later. He'll be starving, George. Ready for his dinner, poor boy. We'll have some ham with it. And cabbage. Bit of a treat," says Eleanor.

"How come I get the drudgery? Not get to do the fancy things?" asks Ellen.

"That's not true. It's just I need to do a lot of beating this afternoon. Pat this butter my way."

Ellen watches as her mother reverts to disparate parts, to the image of the hands she carries constantly in her mind's eye: capable, practical, loving, sometimes cruel, butter-making

129

hands. With them she scoops evenly sized portions of the pale, fluffy butter out of the churn and places them – one by one – on the rimmed side of the pat. Then she takes the other pat and slams it down on top of the butter mound. Now it's in her control. She slaps and whacks the butter, with the vertical faces, with the horizontal faces, moulding it, shaping it, bullying it into the end product she's satisfied with. And on she goes, a one-woman assembly line, until every last lump of butter has been beaten up, until they're dozens of identical squares, with the corners knocked off, arranged on the trestle table.

"There," she says. "Good job done. Now be all fancy if you like. Do the pressing."

"Well thank you, Mother. How honoured I am."

"No need to be clever like that, Ellen. I am your mother, remember."

"How can I forget," she says as she walks over to the trestle with the memory of her father solid in her hands.

She starts on the left and works her way along the row, leaving the impressions of countless four-leafed clovers in the soft butter. With every stamp, she's hoping that for once there'll be some good luck ahead.

Chapter 18

Dusk has descended by the time George arrives home after finishing his shift at four. It's the lack of natural light he's going to miss most, getting up in the dark, coming home in the dark, day in, day out, through these long drawn-out winter months. Thank God for the Sabbath. At least there'll be Sundays off, he thinks. And by March the days will be pulling out as Elizabeth says, lighter earlier, dark later. By June it will still be light at eleven. He wonders what will have happened by June: he'll have moved out and be in digs, he knows that; Jack will be married to Annie; but what about Ellen? God knows where she'll be.

He scrubs himself red-raw in the zinc bath in the outhouse. The black anthracite dust has impacted into what seems like every pore of his skin. It's ingrained in the palms of his hands, lodged deep under his manicured nails, attached to the hairs in his nostrils. It's there in the frothy foam he tries to get off his chest. The taste of carbon lies long in the back of his gullet. On the surface of the water and around the rim, the scum remains thick after he gets out and rubs himself down. He enjoys the roughness of the towel on his skin, it gets the circulation going again. Despite the almost freezing temperature outside, he's glowing.

Once he's dressed – clean singlet and collarless shirt – he walks back to the kitchen where the table's been set as though for a king: best cloth, best china, even spoons hinting at a pudding.

"What's all this in aid of, Mother?" he asks.

"What?" asks Eleanor, smiling. "It's nothing. Just we had a nice drop of buttermilk, so we thought we'd make a meal of it, didn't we, Ellen?"

"Didn't get this treatment even when I came all the way across the Atlantic. Still, you deserve it, I suppose. Sit down. Must have had a tough day," says Ellen.

"Even I'm joining you at the table tonight," says Elizabeth as she taps her way towards the others, who, apart from Eleanor, are already seated. "Worked up quite an appetite sitting on my backside on that settle all day."

With an air of triumph, Eleanor brings the ham she's cooked to mark the occasion to the table on a china platter; the pale pink meat is flaking off the bone. There'll be no problem carving this, she thinks. The smell of cabbage that's been boiling interminably on the hob is thick in the air. And the tureen is piled high with mashed potatoes, moist and golden with the buttermilk.

"I'll say grace," says Eleanor. "And then you can all tuck in:

"'For what we are about to receive, may the Lord make us truly thankful.' Amen."

"Amen," chants the family in unison. All except Ellen.

She sits tight-lipped. Doesn't feel thankful at all. Worked her bloody socks off for this, she thinks. Nothing to do with God.

George talks without coming up for air between mouthfuls. There's so much to say. In a ten-hour stint he feels he already knows all there is about life at level 4 in the seam under the Loughor.

"Too right, it's cramped. Got to duck your head all the time. Feel like the roof's closing in on you. And wet. You can hear the water. Drip. Drip. Drip. Like torture, it is, running down the walls, along the floor. Cold wet, if you know what I mean. Seeps right into you. Funny to think that you're down there, in the bowels of the earth, like a rat – hundreds of them down there – and up above there's the river, right on top of you."

"Can't think about you down there," says Eleanor. "Not natural."

"And it's not that deep when you think about it, really – not like some pits with the winding gear – but still: another world."

Jack is silent, taking every word in but not knowing how to respond. He pretends to lose himself in the cutting and the chewing of what's on his plate. He knows he'll be suffering with indigestion shortly, burning acid constantly regurgitating in his throat, brought on by a mix of fast eating, the buttermilk and a double portion of guilt.

"Kids, a lot of them are. Boys pretending to be men. Not even fluff on their faces. No place for children," goes on George.

"No place for anyone, if you ask me," says Ellen, though she knows they had no choice. "And for a pittance. All those owners getting rich quick and not caring one iota for conditions and safety."

"Don't start now, Ellen," says Eleanor. You know the rule. No politics or religion around the table."

"Let the maid talk," interjects Elizabeth. "She's right, you know."

"That's it, Gran," says Ellen, laughing. "You need to come to the table more often, stir things up a bit."

"Well, it's certainly no place for a woman," says George.

"What the heck do you mean by that? If there's kids there, why not women? Not that I'm advocating it, mind. I stick by what I say: no place for anyone, the way people are treated," says Ellen.

"Don't know where you get your ideas from Ellen, all that going on inside you. No wonder you get those headaches," says Eleanor. "Men have to make a living somehow or other."

"You'd have to cover those ears of yours if you were down there, Ellen. Take it from me, the language is something even you'd be shocked by. Coarse, it is. Cursing and cussing, eff'ing and blinding. Every other word. Altogether different from above ground. Men's talk. Fit only for men and the pit ponies. Thank God their blinkers hide a lot of what goes on," says George.

"Boys will be boys," says Ellen with a sneer.

"Leave it there, now, you lot," says Jack. "Upsets my stomach, all this."

"Yes, do as Jack says, he's the man of the house now," Ellen continues.

"Stop it," shouts Eleanor. "I've gone to a lot of effort with all this. Don't let's spoil things. All I care about is that George keeps safe. There's been a lot of boys not come home from out there, what with the fire-damp and the rushes."

"Don't worry, Mother. I'll look after myself," Ellen snaps, sarcastically, "Just let's enjoy this together now."

"Anyway, thought you *sinners* were planning to go and see that Evan Roberts preach?" interjects Elizabeth, trying to veer the conversation onto a different track.

"We still are, Gran," says Ellen. "It's just that he's been in Liverpool converting the masses. Or so they say. But he's back now. Read it in *The Cambrian*. Like a nasty rash all over the front page. He's back in Moriah, Loughor, soon, on his own patch, so I say we should go next Saturday, after you finish your shift and get spruced up, George. Make a night of it."

"Well, I hope and pray he can do something with you all, especially you, Ellen," says Eleanor.

"We'll see..." Ellen smirks. "We'll see."

Chapter 19

It's almost eight o'clock at night by the time they are well on their way to Loughor in the pony and trap, the twins up front, Ellen and Annie at the rear. By now the full moon is risen, suspended high over the River Loughor, bathing it in a pale, orange light. In the mist, the man in the moon is fuzzy around the edges, wearing a hazy halo.

The tides run fast here, and tonight – with a big spring tide on the flow – minute by minute the River Loughor is swelling. Soon the estuary river will be gulped whole by the advancing sea.

"D'you think it's true what people say, that at one time, at low tide, there used to be stepping stones you could use to cross?" says Annie.

"Who knows what the truth is?" says Ellen. "Nice story, though, Annie. Would make life a lot easier, that's for sure."

But tonight Annie's fanciful stories irritate her and she wonders what she herself believes in any more. She wonders why it's the man in the moon and not the woman in the moon. Wonders why on earth she's on her way to see a man preach about someone, something, she doesn't believe in; hear him talk in the Welsh language even though she only knows a few words. But she's intrigued to find out what all the fuss is about, and desperate to be part of all that's happening.

She thinks back to her time in Sunday School: she'd been such an earnest little child then, all dressed up in her Sunday best – at least as best as was possible in the circumstances. She'd gone to Matins at eleven o'clock with the whole family, Sunday School at half-past two and back again for Evensong at six in the packed church on the village green. Hard to put her finger on the exact time she started to question it all: perhaps her early teens, when she felt her thinking change, her emotions surge, when she began to question whether a so-called God created Man or Man, for whatever reason, created God. And now she's off to a Welsh-speaking *chapel* to be part of the action, as were all the youngsters. To see what it's about – despite her mother's scornful face, with Church written all over it, as they'd left Mount Pleasant.

Jack steers the trap across the stone-arched Island Bridge, over the muddy pills filling fast with the incoming tide, and soon they're rounding the bend, hugging the track towards Loughor. They're heading for the Castle Inn, where they're calling for Hannah.

It's another world here: the streets crawling with people on the move. Men in work clothes coming off shift from the pits and the tin and steel works, their faces grimy and pinched, walking in groups, chatting. And men all washed and changed, walking arm in arm with their wives along the pavements. The only thing that stays still is the smoke from the chimneys of the tightly packed terraces and the tall stacks.

"Well, it's not Hoboken, this," she says.

No-one in the trap responds to her musings.

"Especially that little bridge," she says as they skirt the river where the great timber edifice – by Loughor standards – spans the bloated river, the piles, reinforced with wrought iron, staked deep into the oozing mud, and stone walls as thick as those of the nearby Roman castle abutting the river bank.

"No need to be like that," says George, "it's a fine structure."

Ellen puts their silence and lack of interest down to a kind of fear. She's not been home that long, but long enough to gather that no one was really interested in her life since she'd left Llanrhidian. It amazed her at first, that lack of wanting to know, really know, what a new life in a country half way across the world was like for a young woman on her own. She thought herself gutsy, happy to rise to new challenges, but they closed their ears at her attempts to tell a few stories. They even looked bored on occasion. Then she realised it wasn't boredom, but fear. They didn't want to hear about the new, here where the old stayed unchanged, perhaps forever. They didn't want to know that there was a different way forward, that people were living their lives in different ways, women were daring to think different thoughts. It must make her family feel inadequate. But she understands that her life has already changed forever. That she'll never again be the woman she was at nineteen when she left with ten pounds in her purse. She'll never be the woman who irons the shirts or shines the shoes of a husband, toffing himself up for the pub, like her mother used to do at the beginning, as Annie will probably do, too.

Jack pulls the trap to a halt as they look up and put their hands over their ears as a train loaded with trucks of anthracite steams across the track above the timber arches. They feel the trap shudder with the din, the rumble travelling up through the soles of their feet and echoing in the cavities of their chests.

"Don't know how it stays up," says Annie. "Or how they managed to build it in the first place. Mystery to me."

"It's called engineering," says Ellen. "Engineering."

And, for just as long as it takes the train to cross the bridge, and for the steam to disappear, she thinks of Hoboken and Rutherford and Richard.

Charlie is behind the front bar of the Castle, but apart from a couple of old men playing dominoes and a couple playing skittles in the corner, it is empty. George looks through the hatch into the snug, where there's a fire burning, but apart from that there's no life at all.

"Quiet, tonight?" says Jack. "Where is everybody?"

"Quiet every bloody night," says Charlie. "Don't talk. She's out the back," he tells the group as they pass through the bar, not knowing what to say. "Sorry about the swearing, girls."

Hannah's sitting in a spindle-backed chair in front of the range, her legs raised on a footstool. Ellen notices how puffy her sister's ankles are, how round and pale her face. The woman in the moon springs to mind. Hannah's gold wedding band is cutting into her sausage-like fingers and she has her arms folded across the ledge of her ever-swelling belly. It couldn't be much longer now, judging by the look of her.

"You look done-in, sis," says George. "You all right?"

"Be glad when this is over," she says, patting her mound. "Worn out."

"Change of scenery will do you good," says Ellen. "Your idea, after all."

"I won't be joining you tonight," says Hannah. "Wish I could have let you know in time after your postcard came with the arrangements. Could have saved you the trip."

"We've hardly gone out of our way," says Jack.

"And it's lovely to see you again," says Annie.

"Are you ill?" asks Ellen, sensing something more.

"Not ill, just – you know – a bit fed up. Only natural, I suppose."

"Well, I wouldn't know about that, would I?" says Ellen. "But you look more than a bit fed up to me."

"Shh!" says Hannah, putting her fat finger to her lips and looking towards the door to the bar. "Keep your voices down. Don't want to upset him even more."

"What's the matter with him, then?" asks Ellen.

"Well, look at it in there. Hardly a soul in after work any day of the week. And tonight's Saturday. It's like the grave. He's worried to death. And angry."

"Not with you, I hope," says Ellen.

"No, not me. But he wouldn't be happy with me coming with you to Moriah. Not when the local preacher is the cause of it all."

"It's not your fault," says Ellen.

"Just feel like it would be, if I went against him and came.

Don't want to make matters worse. Fan the flames. Know what he's like."

"What d'you mean by that? And no, I don't know what he's like. He's not cruel to you, is he?"

"Fiery, that's all. He doesn't hit me. Don't worry."

"He'd better not," say the twins together.

"There's other ways to be cruel," says Ellen. "Take it from me."

"Be better once this baby comes," says Hannah, caressing her abdomen subconsciously.

"Is *this* what it's all about?" asks Ellen, raising both her palms to the heavens in exasperation, just as her father used to in the veg patch. "*This?*" she repeats as she turns to leave. She feels the spirit of who she once knew as the young and single Hannah leaving her, just as her father left her, dissipating; dissolving. Ellen looks at Hannah locked in her chair, being swallowed whole by Charlie, the coming baby, obligation. Is *this* what married life and motherhood does to you? Is *this* something she'll ever be capable of? She feels like an outsider, of different stock and blood, helpless in the confines of the seemingly cosy living room, watching her sister being rubbed out in front of her eyes. So full of new life, yet empty.

"Come on, boys. Let's go," she says.

"Calm down, sis. You're like a flippin' virago," says Jack.

Chapter 20

They hear the music before they see the crowds at Moriah. Its strains carry from the open double-door of the chapel: young girls' soprano voices soaring through the Loughor night. Angelic but sad. A lament in the familiar minor key. Ellen had forgotten about the Welsh and their love of self-pity while she was in Hoboken. Welsh misery and maudlin-ness, she'd jokingly referred to it before she'd gone. Why be happy when you could be sad? But what with the scene with Hannah, and the power of the minor key, it is all back. It causes an automatic internal response akin to the feeling of being scooped out and a longing for something that she's not sure of anymore. Inside her head, she can sometimes hear herself crying.

She shoves through the throngs surrounding the chapel, spilling into the graveyard, filling up the pavements. The singing is louder now; even more plaintive. Ellen can hear the well-known Welsh hymn resounding: *dyma gariad fel y moroedd*. She knows this one of old, even though she's Church, as her mother would have it. She's read about it in *The Cambrian*, how it's become what the paper calls 'the love song of the revival', and how it's taken on a brand new meaning. As she stands listening, she's moved to the core by the emotion it carries and beauty in the sounds of the language. Not her mother tongue. But she doubts whether she'll find what its message promises; that she'll find God and 'love as vast as the ocean'. Her feeling is that she'll not be taken in by an ex-collier and a so-called preacher called Evan Roberts, as they all step over the threshold and manage to find spaces in a hard wooden pew at the back of Moriah.

The three female songbirds are right up at the front, at the side of the sêt fawr, next to the grand carved pulpit, raised on high. Probably to the glory of men rather than the glory of God, Ellen thinks, as she sits wedged between Annie and George on the austere pews at the back. Designed to keep the congregation uncomfortable, these, no doubt. Keep them in place. Servile. Eager to do penance. Beg for forgiveness.

She shifts from side to side as much as she can and strains her neck ahead and over the rows and rows of penitents to try and focus on these little songstresses. Just young girls. Younger than her, by the looks of them. Quite plain, too, if she is honest. Yet not in drab clothes, as she'd expected, but dressed to the nines in fancy skirts and frilly silk blouses. Their faces – tilted with contorted feigned piety, their eyes over-sympathetic – are at odds with their outfits. Their look proclaims they have Christianity: something you don't have. As if you'd want it. Well, she doesn't anyway. She knows she's unusual in this respect – here in Wales, at least. But she's already made up her mind. She will not be drawn in to all this business. She's more concerned with equality and fairness. The politics of it all. She's seen women like her coming together and marching for it in America and it's this that stirs her soul. Women from all over the world leading, not following like these.

But fair dos, this soul-saver man must have some power to command all this adoration. For this trio to be part of his Revival entourage, bursting their little lungs and getting all hot and bothered and flushed, singing and praising the Lord, following him like faithful puppies throughout the land. Part of a show, most likely. A travelling circus.

But these young women are oblivious to the congregation. Ellen is fidgeting on her seat while all apart from her in this great big hallowed space sit utterly motionless on the torturing benches. She shifts her gaze to the pews across the aisle. All the heads are facing forwards. Rapt. Duped, more like. Why is she not affected by all this? My God, Annie's got that look in her eyes. And Jack. Even George. She's read somewhere about mass hysteria and people of all persuasions and intellects who have been taken in by music hall acts: clever hypnotists that can put the whole audience under their spell in a few carefully chosen words or a click of the fingers.

And the main act's not even arrived yet.

Religion. Ellen just doesn't understand either the obedience or obsequiousness it seems to require. This search for something bigger. Or perhaps she does. A quick fix. Soothing ointment for a broken heart or a broken spirit or a soul worn out with too many children and not enough to eat and not knowing where the next penny's coming from or the next meal and whether your kids will survive and working your fingers to the bone – if you can find work, that it is – in places not fit for a dog or being abused by men who don't care a jot about you, only about the job you do and the money you make for them. It's not God these people need to turn to, that won't sort things. It's politics. Voices being heard. The old. The sick. The poor. Women, for goodness sake. Getting things changed. Not sinking to the ground on crooked arthritic knees and begging forgiveness for things you aren't responsible for. As though kneeling will change things. It's all a trick, Ellen wants to shout. A quack. Moriah's Medicine Man. Can't you see through it, you people? You deserve better than this.

Every pew is taken, crammed end to end with men and women and children waiting for the main man to make his entrance after the warm-up act finishes. Behind Ellen, people are standing ten-deep, filling the space between the back pews and the entrance. Even the aisles are full to the gunnels, stuffed with silent expectation that charges the atmosphere like invisible static. She can't deny she feels excited too, but doubts she will succumb. More than anything she's feeling hot. The chapel is stifling, airless and sour-smelling from the crush of what must be five hundred stale and sweating bodies. She removes one of her gloves and begins to fan her face fiercely but it does little to stir the air. There's not even the slightest hint of a draught that she usually associates with austere and comfortless religious buildings.

"You all right?" whispers George. "Look a bit peaky."

"Hot, that's all."

"And me," says Annie. "Feel as if I might faint."

"Save that till later, till the spirit moves you," says Ellen.

Can't understand why you're taking the name of the Lord in vain. Why you're so dismissive," says Annie.

"Shhh, you two," says Jack. "He's coming."

As though in a carefully choreographed scene, the whole congregation turns as one to the chapel door to await the entrance of the great man, the way they would to greet the arrival of a royal bride or the Queen of Sheba. But here there is no swell of the organ, no loud trumpet; just silence and a tingling expectation.

Ellen turns with the rest of the people gathered here but all she can see is a slight man in a grey suit with a face the same colour. He is drowning in a sea of people. How on earth will he get to the pulpit? Lo and behold, the problem is solved and the little man is hoisted high by the men in the aisles and passed like a parcel, shoulder to shoulder, from the back to the front until he finds his rightful position. She squints to see him make his way up to the lofty heights of the pulpit. Nearer to God. He looks so fragile, like a solitary leaf in autumn, dwarfed and overpowered by the heavy carvings and the ornate wooden scrolls.

She's expecting some bible-thumping and pulpit-bashing as is the way with these new-fangled denominations. She's read that he can whip up the crowds. But as she watches him, she sees that he seems somewhere else, that he's struggling to find words and get going. Perhaps he's waiting for God's words to seep into him, she thinks, like a medium at a séance. Perhaps he'll vomit them out like ectoplasm. She wonders why she is so cynical about this man – about every man, perhaps. She'll give him a chance. See if he'll live up to all the talk. After all, the congregation is waiting silently for the preacher to do his business.

He begins – gently at first – the way a front sometimes moves in off the horizon: just a ruffle in the air, a slight shift in light, in mood, nothing significant. He is hesitant, taking longer than Ellen thinks normal between his utterances about what she imagines to be the overreaching love of God. Uncoordinated. The odd stutter. A ramble. But then he's into his flow, as when the storm is directly overhead and the wind from the south west is raging and the rain is lashing.

The congregation is moved.

Ellen listens as he starts to speak in what is called 'tongues', and to call for what she reads about in the news and thinks must be an appeal for souls. It seems that most are ready to part with them. The decibels are rising and he's urging everyone present to confess their sins and put away their doubts, to obey the holy spirit in all spheres. Then both his arms are raised heavenward and he's urging and welcoming them all to come to Christ. Here. Now. In public. In Loughor on a late Saturday night.

This man might have notched up one hundred thousand souls for God, but he's not having hers. Not a chance. But the tally is rising in Moriah along with the mumblings and the mutterings of hundreds of individual prayers.

Ellen feels the urge to clamp her hands over her ears to block out the din of the men, women and children, confessing

147

to sins they haven't committed and asking for God's forgiveness when they've done nothing wrong. Their faces are twisted in pain and they're on their knees begging on the unforgiving splintered floor.

She glances at George, but he doesn't return her eye contact. He's already taken. Incoherent English words are spewing from his mouth, and he's holding his lovely hands over his chest. And Annie, too. She's quieter, on her young knees at her side, her freckled face pale as though she's going down with something serious. Her lips look dry and colourless and saliva is caked white at the corners. Surely not Jack, Ellen thinks, not worldly, pragmatic, foul-mouthed, ale-loving Jack. But his head's down, oblivious to the world, chuntering on about the darkness and crying for the light to come into his life and confessing all his known sins, his fist clenched and beating his chest in time with every syllable. What the hell has he done in his seventeen years to have this burden pressing down on him?

Her dead father's face comes to her. In his beloved veg patch, praying for something in his peculiar way, his arms opened up to the heavens. Perhaps this might have been his salvation. Too late now.

She can stand it no longer. The din. The discordance. The cacophony of an orchestra that is badly out of tune. The heat and anxiety is sapping and she feels breathless. *Plyg fi, Arglwydd,*[*] the row of supplicants in front is begging in unison. They have moved from one state to another, from

---

[*] *Plyg fi, Arglwydd* – Bend me, Lord.

where they were to some place new. And they're bent low, like trees felled in a Gower storm, so low they're almost prostrate.

Now her lungs are bursting, not with a lust for religion as are these poor people here, gasping for God. Nor for Evan Roberts himself as are the trio at the front. Ellen is gasping for oxygen. With that there is the sound of breaking glass as one of the windows is smashed by a man in the far corner, seeking to get some ventilation and break the oppressive heat. Through it rushes the cool breath of fresh air and life. And it fills her heart and soul.

Chapter 21

Spring surprises everyone with its early arrival. By the beginning of March the snowdrops in the garden at Mount Pleasant have already died back and, pushing up in their place, are crocus and primroses. Wild daffodils yellow the verges beneath the budding hedgerows, heads held high and trumpeting loudly of warmer days to come. Even some of the ewes in the top fields have lambed early. They need keeping an eye on. Things look full of promise if not certainty.

"I'll give you a hand if you like," Ellen says to Jack over breakfast.

"Aye. Be good to have some company up there. Lonely old job, sometimes."

"Yes. Get out from under my feet for a few hours," says Eleanor. "Going to start on the spring cleaning. Open the windows. Get some air through. Need to get everything ship-shape here before I go to Loughor."

Ellen and Jack step out into the yard. In the shed, they reach for the crooks and set off for the fields at Welsh Moor. This morning they make a sad pair as Ellen is very much aware of what Jack is thinking. That he's lost a father. His brother has left the farm in all but body. It's all on him now. Just a sister hanging on and God knows how long she'll stick around. There'd been so many of them once, in lambing season.

With the climb to the higher fields, the breeze is stronger yet carries a gentle whisper of warmth and things to come. Ellen takes off her hat, stuffs it into her coat pocket, unpins her hair and shakes it free, letting the wind run through it. She turns her face to the sun and lets it permeate her skin, seep into her cold winter-bound bones. This is what spring should mean, she thinks. Renewal. This is revival.

Jack unties the baling cord that is securing the rickety old gate into their field adjacent to the moor. He heaves it up with his right shoulder to take its weight, lifts it so that it opens, despite its rusty, broken hinges. Everything around here is flaking and rusted or encrusted with salt, thinks Ellen. Struggling to keep intact through a winter of wet and an incessant wind off the sea. She takes a look at Jack as if to prove a point to herself. He's young now, but he'll bend like the trees around here soon enough, bow in the middle to the will of the south westerlies like the stunted blackthorn that stoops at an angle of forty-five degrees around the perimeter of the field. There's an inevitability about it that makes her shiver despite the rays of sunlight.

Under the blackthorn, along the edges of the field, most of the new lambs are suckling, but in the middle there's a heap of fleece stained red, strewn across the pasture, and a magpie beaking what's left of a carcass, bobbing its head and slurping out the entrails. Nearby, a still-born lamb, its eyes pecked out, the sockets hollow.

"Pity, that," says Jack as he hefts the weight of the dead ewe and lamb to the side. "Dig a pit, now. Can't expect anything else, really. Not this early."

"But still, the others are doing all right," says Ellen, wondering whether Jack's life would have panned out differently if he'd been born with a caul over his face, whether he'd have some luck or free choice as the eldest son on a farm. As might Richard.

She watches a young lamb jerk to its feet and latch on to its mother. She thinks about Hannah and the baby coming any day soon. She thinks about herself. Her periods are coming every month now. She's sick and tired of death and this place that feels like it's in its death throes too.

When he's finished the digging, they tramp the field, checking the ewes that are still pregnant. There are still about twenty ready to drop, heavy in the girth, shit-spattered, worm-ridden and most limping with foot rot and oozing with mange. Jack wrenches a few free from the brambles and they run off, trailing the green and prickly foliage that's attached to their fleeces. It never ceases to amaze Ellen how lambs can change into such stupid, ugly creatures. It's here in the top fields that she knows she made the right decision in leaving for America. That life in this place will never be for her. Not anymore.

"Right. That'll do it for now," says Jack. "Check them again in the morning."

"You go back, then. Fancy staying out a bit longer. Blow the cobwebs away," says Ellen.

"You be all right on your own?"

"Course. Going to carry on up over Welsh Moor and do a loop back to the house. I always loved it up there. Catkins. Pussy Willow. Chirrup of birds."

"And Richard!"

"Go on. Be off with you. See you later."

Happy to be alone, out in the air, Ellen retraces the steps she's taken a thousand times before, along the narrow twisting track that skirts Cil Ifor Tops and the iron age ditches and up to Parc-y-Rhedyn Farm. It's always colder here in this position at the summit of the hill, fearlessly catching the wind from all directions. Ellen likes the bleakness of it all. For a few minutes, she stops to catch her breath, to listen to the wind as it whines through the leafless trees that seem to cower in submission.

It's not far from here to Prysg Farm: it's just around the bend and down the lane, tucked into a hollow on the left before the moor opens up. She will walk past, eyes forward, head held high. It won't take long. Minutes, at most. Then she can breathe easy again.

As she rounds the corner, and the sound of the wind drops, she hears the rhythmic thud of wood against wood. She knows it's him. Richard. Has to be. Making the most of the precocious weather to get out and get things in order. She cannot be certain of where the sound is coming from. Difficult to tell. Perhaps from the yard at Prysg. The woods beyond. She carries on, face flushed. Her breath comes quickly, and that's not solely attributable to the fresh air and the incline. She quickens her pace in the false logic of getting it over with sooner rather than later. Either way, perhaps, there will be an encounter.

The noise is louder, monotonous: the dull thud, thud, thud of a mallet against a stake. And from the top of the lane she sees him at the side of the bank of earth and stone, swinging his mallet against the heads of blackthorn stakes. He can't see her. He's immersed in the laying of this flying hedge. Ellen can see that he's already banged in a line of vertical uprights where gaps have appeared in the old hedge. Livestock has no doubt been getting through in both directions. She is a silent spectator, hypnotised by the rhythm of the sound and the sight of his body in motion. The sheer beauty of the movement. The firmness of the thighs and legs planted in the ground like sturdy oaks, as though he has grown there. The strength in the upper body which looks tough and solid, as though – were she to press it with her fingers – it would be tough: resistant, unyielding, hard flesh. Yet there is a grace in the action that is almost balletic, displaying a caring sensitivity to the task in hand.

She waits. She watches. He wipes his brow with the back of his hand, oblivious to everything apart from the staking and binding and creation of this barrier that will do its job. She can smell the sap from the freshly split blackthorn on the breeze. She inhales deeply.

She's too far away to see the detail, but she remembers the sinewy forearms, the little muscle shaped like an egg that would appear by his elbow when he clenched his fist. He could make it appear. Disappear. Appear. Disappear. A magician.

The veins standing proud on the back of his hands, his wrists. The fair hair downy against the weathered skin. The strong fingers. How they felt entwined in hers. Sometimes the butterfly touch of his long dark eyelashes on her cheek.

She feels rooted to the spot. She wants her feet to stride past him, but they won't budge. Her knees are all a-wobble. There's a new feeling arising from deep inside. She's not experienced it before. Never. It's a feeling that is separate from those in her head – her reasoning – from anywhere above her eyebrows. This is most definitely a below-the-eyebrows feeling, a below-the-waist feeling. But it's deeper than desire for his body and his sex. It is lodged so deep that she feels like groaning like an ewe in labour. Something is bubbling up like lava, turning her insides to liquid. Giving her an unashamed primitive urge to squat down in the ditch at the side of this country lane and raise her skirt, drop her drawers, bear down and grunt and wail and pant and push and push and push until she births Richard's baby. And it takes her breath away.

Chapter 22

Hold the fort is the command Eleanor issues before she takes leave of Mount Pleasant for Hannah's confinement at Loughor. From the yard, Ellen waves her off until her arm aches, keeping waving long after as she disappears from view in the trap, with Jack at the reins. If she stops waving too soon, she fears her mother might not really be gone, might come back.

Ellen would like to go to Hannah to support her too, see her bring that new life into the world, sniff the scalp of the little bundle, but Eleanor has decreed that she can't be spared from the farm.

"It needs a woman here," she's said. "What with the boys out all day and her in the corner, there. They need something put in front of them."

After the sighting of Richard, Ellen has lost the stomach for food and any fight. She is beginning to wonder if there might indeed be something in Elizabeth's motto of "say nothing's best, maid" as a means to an uncomplicated life. If she's honest, despite disagreeing that the foundations of the stone walls of Mount Pleasant will crumble unless she fills everyone's bellies with food, churns the butter, launders the clothes or wipes every speck of dust free from every visible surface, she's happy to have some breathing space away from her mother. Richard has got under her skin again and she is sure that her mother can see him inhabiting her. The see-sawing moods. The flashes of temper. The longing, even. "Can read you like a book, my girl. Written all over your face." Yes, it's better like this: mother there, me here, she thinks.

She can get a lot done in a couple of weeks. She vows to use the time profitably while she has the house to herself, so to speak, as despite the boys and Elizabeth being permanent fixtures, she is looking forward to the absence of that feeling her mother somehow creates in her: as if the life is being sucked clean out of her.

With six weeks to go until the wedding of Jack and Annie at St. Illtyd and St Rhidian's, she's invited Annie around on Ellen's first day free of Eleanor, so that they can make a start on her own bridesmaid's dress. She hates the title, *bridesmaid*, but considers that *maid-of-honour* or, heaven forbid, *matron-of-honour* would be even worse. She's never been a bridesmaid before and hopes that she'll never have to be again: the dress, the flowers, being an adjunct to the person who will be the centre of attention. It's just not her style. Especially the ridiculous dress and rigmarole. But it's little Annie and Jack's day, so she'll keep her mouth closed and show willing.

Despite the fact that soon Annie will be living in Mount Pleasant, she comes to the front door. Ellen opens it to see her loaded down with a basket and parcels.

"Here. Let me give you a hand. Should have come round

the back and walked in. No need to knock," says Ellen taking the parcel from Annie.

"Didn't like to. Not yet," says Annie, smiling shyly at her and nodding to Elizabeth in the corner.

Apart from the fact that the big, green bow in her hair has gone and the ringlets are now soft curls, Annie looks hardly any different than she did in her school days: complexion pale and peppered with sunspots, wholesome and healthy. And happy. Wide-smiled and little even teeth with a gap between the front two. She's going to make a beautiful bride without much effort.

Annie takes her large dressmaking shears from the basket and snips the string of one parcel, which she's placed on the kitchen table. She undoes the outer brown paper to reveal soft tissue paper and inside that, carefully folded fabrics and a cut-out image.

"I saw this in a periodical. What d'you think?" she asks.

Ellen appears interested and pours over the black and white sketch of a woman in a fashionable wedding dress.

"Beautiful," she says. "Very you. Not too fussy and not overwhelming, if you know what I mean."

"D'you think so? You're right. I'm not very tall and I didn't want to be swamped by fabric."

"You're petite. Delicate. Uncomplicated."

"Only a short train. Neat sleeves."

"And a tiny waist. I've never had a tiny waist. Cart horse, me."

"No, you're not. Strong, you are. Inside and out. Anyway,

this is the fabric – ivory satin and Battenburg lace – not too much – and just a little ribbon around the waist," she says, rapt, sensuously stroking the material with her palm as she would a cat.

"God, Annie. I didn't know there were so many types of fabric. Mostly wool, me," laughs Ellen, brushing down her drab skirt. "So what about your head? The veil?"

"Simple tulle. Spring flowers. Nothing fancy."

"Lovely. You're going to look a picture. Now what about me? What can you turn me into?"

"Well, what d'you think of this?" she says, snipping open the other parcel.

Annie unfolds the swatch of green fabric and lays it out on the table.

"Green? Feared I'd have to have some frothy lace too..." says Ellen, relieved.

"Thought this taffeta was you. It's too warm for velvet. This has a lovely sheen. Will really suit you with your dark hair."

"And you!"

"And me!"

"I really like it. Not just saying that, but I really do. But what about the cost?"

"Father's paying. It's fine."

"That's kind of him," says Ellen. "Nice to be able to do that for your daughter's wedding."

"I just need to measure you, now. Then I can make some patterns and cut out the fabric when I get home. I'll come back for a fitting when I've tacked it up."

"The very thought of doing that makes me heave," says Ellen.

"Yes. I haven't forgotten you and sewing and the needle through the finger in school."

"Give me cooking any day. But not needlework. I'd rather suck my own blood!"

"Don't take after your mother, then? Marvellous seamstress, my mother tells me she is."

"Just clickety-clacks, crochets and darns these days. Can't remember the last time I saw her actually make something, create something new. But d'you know, you've just put an idea into my head."

"Really?"

"Yes. I need to think it through and talk something over with Mother but I think I might have something you might both be interested in, when the time comes."

Ellen stands on the rug in front of the range, takes off her white blouse, her dark skirt, and stands shoeless in her chemise, drawers and stockings. Carefully, Annie unrolls her tape measure and starts jotting down the measurements in her little book with the blacklead. Bust: 36 inches; Waist: 27 inches. Hips: 38 inches. Underarm to wrist: 22 inches. Nape of neck to floor: 55 inches.

"Squat, I am. Stocky like the Evanses. Short waisted and low-kneed, according to her on the settle," says Ellen.

"I heard that, maid. Every word," laughs Elizabeth. "Keep your chitter-chatter down if you don't want me to take notes."

"Have you finished the guest list, then?" whispers Ellen. "Can't be easy, that!"

"All done. About fifty. Just family and close friends. Parish Hall. Thought I'd tell you that Richard is on the list. Well, you know, he's been close to Dad, and Tom and him are about the same age... you don't mind, do you?"

"Mind? No. Not at all," says Ellen.

She can feel a flush across her chest and neck, which must be visible to Annie above the chemise.

"He's coming on his own. Still not courting."

"Shame he's on his own," says Ellen flatly so that Annie can't take the meaning from it. "Pity, that."

Chapter 23

After a few days, Ellen feels on a relatively even keel. There's a pattern in the day that she's getting used to: George's lunch box to prepare ahead of his shift; Jack's breakfast to prepare after he's fed the stock and milked the cows; Elizabeth to be kept topped-up with cups of tea, and then the coming together for supper when everyone is back under one roof. There's a quiet of a different kind when her mother's not at home: not the absence of her voice, but the atmosphere is free of tension, like a length of taut rope that has been slackened.

She's not expecting any more visitors so it's a surprise when Eva the Post Office knocks on the door with a letter. She could have dropped it through the letterbox but she wants to deliver it by hand, make sure Ellen gets it.

"It's from America," she says. "Can tell by the fancy envelope. And the stamp."

"Thank you, Eva. Very kind," says Ellen, closing the door swiftly behind her, knowing full well that by the end of the morning, her business will be through the village like a dose of salts.

She walks back to the kitchen, settles herself down to tear open the letter and pore over the contents.

"Who was at the door?" shouts Elizabeth across the room.

"Eva," replies Ellen, wishing her grandmother would leave her in peace.

"What she want, then?"

"Letter," she says, "which I'm trying to read!"

"Nosey bugger."

167, River Avenue,
Hoboken,
New Jersey

8th March, 1905

My dearest Ellen,

I hope this letter finds you well and in good spirits. I do not know what has transpired since you left last December, but whatever has happened, or continues to happen, I trust you are coping. In fact, I know, you'll be coping. As I've said many a time, you're a very capable young woman.

I am coping here (just) without you in the kitchen and keeping this sprawling house in order. We miss you.

As I said before you sailed, you mean a lot to us and your position is still open should you wish to return. But, I can't keep it open indefinitely and as it will be six months in June, perhaps you could write and let us know your plans so I can make arrangements either way. I have taken on a temporary girl meanwhile, a young Irish girl, who's very nice. But she's not you.

Last of the snow has gone and spring has come here to Hoboken. I hope it has with you in Wales and will lift your spirits with summer to look forward to.

With fondest regards,
Mrs. Randall (Edith)

PS. I know your return passage is catered for, but if money is a problem, please let us know and we can sort something out.

Decision time, Ellen thinks, stuffing the letter back in the envelope and into her apron, in the hope that Elizabeth won't interrogate her.

"Who's it from, then?" asks Elizabeth.

"Mrs. Randall. Wants to know if and when I'm going back."

"And? Not much to keep you here now, is there?"

"No. Don't suppose there is," replies Ellen.

She's agitated after this, like an unbroken pony, hoofing around the house with a restless energy. Now Mrs. Randall is forcing her hand when she's not quite ready. She has unfinished business here – with Matthias, and perhaps with Richard too. Her emotions swing from hating him for hurting her so much to feeling sorry that he is still on his father's reins. This is a recent thought, that he is as much a victim of expectation and duty – as the eldest son on a farm – as any would-be wife to bring forth the next generation. And so it has to go on. From generation to generation. Almost biblical. He has much more to lose than she has, perhaps. Much more to keep him here, she supposes. Marriage for him is about much more than love. It's economic; and that's a hard lesson to accept and one that she's already learned to her cost. Again, she hears Matthias' words to her father back then in the kitchen: *With her he'll just get old and then he'll die.*

Chapter 24

On the first Friday of her respite from Eleanor, Ellen is working off her agitation in the dairy: scumming, churning, beating the butter into order, just like her mother does. With every pat, she thinks of Matthias and how she'd like to beat him around the head, leave the impression of the clover in his skull. That would sort him out.

Her desires are interrupted by what she can only call a sense of impending doom. She's had this feeling of deep unsettledness before, she tells herself. It's just an over-active imagination, the need to make decisions. After all, she always has it when she sees Esther the Cats and nothing untoward happens then. Despite the mild air, she feels a chill. She strokes her forearms and notices that the dark hairs are standing on end and there are goosebumps. She pats the butter harder. Faster. Tries to force the feeling out of her system.

She's not as surprised as she should be when she hears a commotion in the yard, a young voice, hollering: "Jack? Jack?"

She bounds into the yard to see young Emlyn from Common Farm in his working clothes, his face black with coal dust, eyes white and frightened.

"What's the matter, Emlyn?"

"Flood."

"Christ," she shouts. "What about George? Is he all right?"

"His chest. Collapsed, he has. We need help."

"Jack's up the quarry, on the lime. Run and get him. Quick. I'll get my coat and some blankets and wait here. Pick me up on the cart on the way back."

"Righto. Be as quick as I can."

"Are there men lost, Emlyn?"

"Aye. Boys mostly, according to the tally man. Three lamp checks unaccounted for," he says, his little face crumpling.

As Ellen, Jack and Emlyn approach New Lynch in the pony and trap, it is silent apart from the sound of the pumps. No men talking. No trams running. Just an eerie stillness. Men – their clothes wet and black – stand at the entrance to the drift, waiting; hoping. Women too, who left what they were doing and ran to the mine, wearing shawls tightly wrapped around them, their faces fearful. Some men lie on the ground on what's left of some sparse grass at the side of the yard. It's hard to tell them apart, as they are black from head to foot, with grimy faces and the sort of wide-eyed stares that follow shock.

They pick out George. He's gasping for air and wheezing, interrupted only by dry coughing spasms. Jack squats down beside him and tells him not to try and talk. Save his breath. It will be all right, he promises. Roughly, Jack pulls his brother's body face down across his lap as you would a baby with wind. He used to see his father do this when they were kids, when George's chest was tight.

"I've got you," he says. "Get you sorted and home in a jiff."

With the outside edges of both palms, Jack pummels George's back in an attempt to clear the airways, get the muck off his chest.

Ellen takes her clean handkerchief and spits on it, then gently wipes the dirt from around George's mouth. She watches him turning blue around the gills, his lips draining of blood. Feeling useless, she stands on the sidelines, picking at the unwanted blankets.

"It's loosening up a treat, George," says Jack, mentally relieved by his physical efforts.

And with that, George heaves and retches white froth tinged with black specks onto the grass beside him.

"See. That's better," says Jack. "Better out than in!"

A bizarre pair, they look to Ellen in her state of panic. Twins. But not the same at all. One black. One white. Jack, cheeky and strong in spirit and constitution. George frailer: gentle and sensitive in soul and body. Life already taking them in different directions.

"C'mon, George. Let's get you back in front of the range. Get you warm. Get some steam in the air," says Ellen.

Later, he sits propped up with pillows in the stick chair in the kitchen, the kettle belching out steam. As he is too weak to bathe, his siblings remove just his work boots and his soaked and blackened outer garments. Gently, Ellen wipes his face, hands and forearms with a flannel, tries to make him look human again. The water in the bowl turns black. He might look like a man on the outside, but there by the range, he is no more than a frightened grimy child, giving himself up to his sister.

"Good job your mother's not here to see you like this, boy," shouts Elizabeth. "She'd have a fit."

"Aye. No point panicking her. Spoiling it all for her. Keep it quiet until she gets back," says Jack. "He'll be fine by then."

Chapter 25

Ellen knows him by his knock. Rat tat-a-tat-tat. Tat tat. On the back door, no less. Cheeky sod. Thinks he can breeze in and out of here just like he had when Father was alive, as if nothing happened. Full of himself, pompous oaf. Just when they're having a bit of peace and quiet, too, after clearing away Sunday dinner.

George still isn't up to much so he's reading in a chair by the range, his head deep between the covers of Dickens; his mind somewhere else. Jack taking time to do some paperwork in the other room on what was William's but is now his desk.

"It's Matthias, maid," announces Elizabeth. "Saw that peaked cap and big head of his go strutting past the window."

"Yes. Recognise his knock. Arrogant. What's he want now, for God's sake?" asks Ellen.

"What d'you think? Chooses his moment with your mother not around. Ready to pounce – get his pickings."

"Well, he's going to get more than he bargained for. Pickings, my foot. Picked the wrong one, here," says Ellen, rising to answer the door.

"Matthias. This is a surprise. Wasn't expecting you," she says, tight lipped but smiling.

"Heard George had a bit of an episode at New Lynch. Terrible business, that."

"He's doing all right though... aren't you, George?" she shouts to George.

"Fine," he says from in front of the range, his feet on the cat, his head moving swiftly back down towards the book to avoid having to talk further.

"Won't you come in a minute?" asks Ellen.

"I won't stop long. Won't keep you. Don't like to intrude," he says as he steps over the threshold without wiping his feet or removing his boots. Just his cap. Ellen pulls the door to.

"How d'you hear about George, then, Matthias?

"Eva!"

"Might have guessed."

"News travels fast around here. Was hoping your mother'd be back by now," he says. "Wanted to have a quiet word."

"Another week, yet. Supposed Eva would have told you. Surprises me, that."

Ellen's voice is taut like an overstrung violin. Confrontation is in the air, in the tightness of her diaphragm. She is centre-stage, the performance about to begin. In the background, she can sense Elizabeth feigning sleep, glances across and sees her eyes closed, her chin on her chest. She can sense George distancing himself, going deeper into his fictional world, his eyes fixed on the words in front of him. But she doesn't hear a page being turned, and neither, from the next room, with the door wide-open, is there a peep from Jack.

"It's the little issue of the land. Thought the time was about right, now," says Matthias, fiddling with the cap in his hands.

"Aah. "About right"; I see. Does that mean Father's cold enough in the grave now for protocol or perhaps that Mother's not here? Just little old me to deal with?" asks Ellen.

"No need to be like that with me, Ellen. I've only come to get what's rightfully mine. Fair and square, it was, you know. He lost it fair and square. So now I need the deeds signed. Handed over. Legal, like."

"Fair and square? Do me a favour, Matthias. Father wasn't well. He was an alcoholic, for Christ's sake. Dying he was, when he did that deal. Not in his right mind."

"He seemed all right when he was in the pub with the men. No need to blaspheme. Take the Lord's name in vain. Not seemly."

"I take it by 'with the men' you mean 'away from the women'? Father's problems were just all for show? Him pretending is a bit like you pretending to be a Christian. Just for some sort of pathetic social standing. And 'seemly'? Me? D'you actually think I care what you think of me, Matthias? After the way you treated me? And how you treated your son, if I'm honest. You're a bully Matthias. You are full of hot air. There. Truth's out."

No one in the room says a word. From the corner comes an extended rattle and exhalation of breath as Elizabeth pretends to dream. From the chair comes the slightest whisper of a page being turned. From the next room comes the exaggerated rustle of papers. Apart from Ellen, who is almost spent now, the room's inhabitants are the epitome of pretence. The cat rouses itself from sleep on the mat, springs to the door and lets out a long miaow, demanding to be let out. Ellen opens the door roughly and puts her foot up its backside to speed things up.

"You too, Matthias. Out! Before I put my foot up your arse as well. I'll be in touch with you shortly about the land. What I intend to do. Just putting the final touches to the plan. I'll make sure to tell Mother you called. Good day."

And with that, cap in hand, he's gone, the kitchen door remaining ajar just long enough to allow a blast of cold fresh air to take the sting out of Ellen's cheeks.

Chapter 26

On her return to Mount Pleasant, Eleanor reminds Ellen of a sheep's bladder that the boys sometimes use as a ball. She looks wrinkled, sagging, utterly deflated. A sorry reminder of what she once was.

She sits in her stick chair by the range, sapped of life. Ellen has the urge to rush to the parlour and reach for the leather bellows that are kept at the ready on the hearth. She sees herself inserting the nozzle into her mother's mouth, taking hold of the handles and squeezing the stream of air into her chest in an attempt to revive her. There she is without oxygen, and there was Matthias – an old windbag – all inflated, as though he were about to take off.

"What's brought all this about, Mother? Thought you'd be overjoyed at the new baby," says Ellen.

"Oh, don't get me wrong, I am," says Eleanor, "he's a beautiful little boy. And good. It's worn me out, that's all. Didn't realise how much being over there would take it out of me."

"Not just the baby, then?"

"No. Not just the baby. It's as miserable as sin there."

"Pub still quiet?"

"Like death. And Charlie worried."

"It'll pass. Be back to normal soon – all this religious fervour's just a fad."

"Anyway, she's made her choice. Didn't like to tell her 'I told you so'. Flippin' publicans!"

"It'll be fine. You mark my words. She's got the little one, now," says Ellen, trying to reassure but not at all convinced by her own words or those of her mother. "We've got to get you back on your feet now."

"It's my nerves. I'm so washed out with everything that's been going on. Feel like I'm ill from the feet up."

In all her twenty-one years, this is the first time Ellen has seen any sign of what her mother would usually call weakness. Always the tough front. The banter. The business. It's difficult for her to witness this: it's as if her mother's shell has been shucked and she's leaking out.

Instinctively, Ellen stoops and wraps her strong forearms around her mother, pressing her face into the pillow of her own bosom until she almost smothers her. Eleanor doesn't resist the unusual gesture: Ellen feels her pliant in her embrace, the tears falling and the heaving of her diaphragm. *There, there*, she finds herself repeating.

Today is not the day to tell her mother of George's brush with death at the mine nor Matthias's unscheduled visit and the spat about the land, and definitely not about the letter from Mrs. Randall.

"I'll get the kettle on," says Ellen. "Put your feet up. You deserve it."

"I do love you, you know. Sometimes I don't like your ways; but I do love you."

"I know you do, Mother. Me too."

"Glad to be home. Nothing like your own bed. Think I'll have a little lie down until the boys get in, if that's all right with you?"

When Jack comes in later from the milking, Ellen double-checks that he hasn't divulged anything about George or Matthias to his mother on the journey back from Loughor.

"Could see she was all in," says Jack. "You told me not to say, anyway."

"Good. Thought you hadn't. She would have mentioned it. You're learning," laughs Ellen. "Warn George too when he gets back. Tell him in the outhouse so he doesn't muck up."

"Will do, boss," replies Jack, winking.

"As for her in the corner, she's been primed already. Isn't that right, Gran?"

"My lips iz sealed, maid," she says, grinning, placing her knobbled index finger to her mouth.

Eleanor's up now, and they're all seated around the table for supper. Even Elizabeth has shuffled to join the family.

"Not used to being waited on, hand and foot," says Eleanor as Ellen paces back and forth to the range and the dresser, fetching and carrying for everyone.

"Well don't get used to it. It's just till we get you back on your feet. Anyway, don't know why the boys can't pull their fingers out. I mean it wasn't as if I, or you, Mother, were born with a predisposition to boil spuds, set the table and stand around all day until everyone's fed and watered, only to do the same thing again at the next meal."

"Don't start on all that, now, Ellen. I just don't have the energy. Want to hear what's been going on."

Ellen glares across the table and fixes her dark eyes on Jack and then George. A stare that says "you wouldn't dare". Just to make sure, she gives each one of them a kick in the shins.

"It's all change at the mine since –" says George.

"Let's *not* talk about the mines," interrupts Ellen, trying to steer the conversation away from any hint of flood or collapse of pit props or George's chest.

"– since the men heard Evan Roberts," continues George. "Can't believe it,"

"Mmmph," says Eleanor. "Responsible for a lot of things that Evan Roberts. Charlie and Hannah's livelihood, for a start. Like a graveyard there, now that men have turned their back on the drink."

"Thought you'd be pleased about that, Mother. Turning away from drink," taunts Jack.

"Well it's not easy for me, is it? Not when it's the future of my daughter – and my grandson now, as well. They've got to put food on the table, after all."

"Nothing's black and white though, is it?" says Ellen.

"No. It's not. It's taken me a long time and I thought I'd never say it but no, it's not," repeats Eleanor.

The family listens, all ears, as George tells them that things

176

are beginning to change underground. Bit by bit, it's becoming a different sort of place. Puts it all down to Evan Roberts.

"Cleaning them up, he is: their tongues, their manners," he says. "Still a man's world, mind, or I should say 'would-be-men', I'll give you that. But it's less foul, less coarse."

George has to give it to the man, he says, he's touched them all, and if things are not quite transformed, they are changing.

"The miracle man from Moriah," quips Ellen. "He'll be feeding the five thousand next. Turning water into wine. Oh. Sorry, forgot. Wine's forbidden."

No one laughs.

George goes on to tell them that the levels are filling with a new kind of gentleness, a change of spirit. "It's a place where a woman would feel comfortable," he says.

"That's a laugh," says Ellen.

He takes no notice of Ellen's sarcasm and laughs at their incredulous reaction when he tells them that the pit ponies don't respond to the refined and blasphemy-free instructions the men give them. Their eyes may be blinkered but their ears are not used to being spared from loud volume and impatient, aggressive imperatives of the four-lettered kind. Now they are supposed to answer to mild and loving requests to walk on, halt, or stand still.

"Like I said, it's just for the time being, not forever," says Ellen.

"O ye of little faith," laughs Jack.

He tells them that lots are giving up alcohol – taking the pledge – and vowing never to let a drop touch their lips again.

No longer do they stay out half the night and come home to beat their women and kids.

"I've heard that judges in the courts are complaining because they don't have any cases to try," says George.

"That'll be the day," says Ellen. "Flash in the pan, it all is. As you two well know, boys will be boys."

George carries on, telling them that the miners are now filled with a thirst for knowledge. They've asked him to read from the Bible or recite poetry while they have a spell and eat from their lunch boxes. They're hungry for food of a different kind, he says.

"So you get to be a poet, after all," teases Jack.

"Yes, I do, actually," says George, blushing. "And at least they enjoy it!"

"Yes, leave him be," says Eleanor. "Done a lot for you, your brother. For the family."

"It's not just what that blessed man's done for others though, is it?" asks Ellen, already knowing the answer. "You're different too, George, since that spectacle at Moriah, " says Ellen.

"Yes. Yes I am."

"And you, Jack," she says turning to him. "Even you."

"Yes. Me too. Same as him, exactly."

"Good God alive," says Ellen. "He got to you two good and proper."

"In fact, we've been thinking," says George, turning to Jack for moral support. "We've decided we're going to take the pledge. Both of us. Before the wedding."

Chapter 27

The hedgerows are bursting into life: cow parsley and horse parsley scent the air, wild mint is beginning to shoot, nettles beginning to sting. In the stream that rushes through the village near the mill, watercress will soon choke the surface. In the lee of the limestone hill, the woods are carpeted with the dense clusters of green foliage and the white blossom of ramsons, the spring-cool air pungent with their distinctive odour.

It's here in the shade of the trees that Eleanor has taken to walking, day after day, stooping low to pick the wild garlic. There was a time when she'd forage for herbs and wild plants to eat; but now she's garnering this plant for other, murkier reasons.

She puts it down to Loughor, the worry of Hannah and the new baby, the fretting about George in the mines, money worries, the land, the uncertainty of Ellen's intentions, the wedding, the change in the boys, the gnawing grief. It's a feeling of growing darkness that's dragging her down into a deep, black well. This mood of restlessness – of fidgeting to keep at bay unwelcome thoughts – prevails not just in her waking hours but in her sleep too, which has become fitful with the intrusion of recurring nightmares of the dead and the disfigured; her hair coming out in clumps in her hands, of her teeth loosening in her slackening gums and falling out. She wonders how it is possible to keep going on such little sleep, understands how lack of it is a torture to the mind and body, how it distorts reality.

Recently, just before dawn when she's poised between sleep and wakefulness, she had hallucinations and out-of-body experiences. In them she becomes detached from her own physical self and is lying in the bed then rising horizontally, floating slowly – as light as dust – to the ceiling.

Once again, she opens up in the kitchen to Ellen about how she feels. How she fears she's going mad, is possessed by evil spirits. She's ashamed that she is weak, has succumbed to her nerves.

"You're not mad, Mother. No madder than you've ever been," Ellen says. "You've had a packet. It's just the mind's normal reaction to too many unusual situations. It's tired."

"Can see how your father took to the swearing and the drink when God didn't do anything to help him," says Eleanor.

"Sometimes any god will do."

"D'you ever feel like this?"

"Sometimes. But it's not like it was. You'll get better, Mother. More good days than bad days again."

"I'm trying ramsons. Don't tell anyone though, will you?"

"Course not. Not eating them, are you? Not raw?"

"No. Just tying them to the bedpost. Keep the demons at bay."

"Like I said. Any god will do. And you need to talk to me. Not bottle it all up."

"I know."

"There's a lot to look forward to, you know. A lot of joy to be had. Though sometimes you can't see it – it'll come."

Eleanor lies in turmoil in the bed, which seems so much larger without William. Her legs seem incapable of stilling. It's not pain, but a constant discomfort as though a million insects are crawling beneath her skin. She places her hands on her calves to see if she can feel the insects moving, but there is nothing to the touch. She attempts to stop the maddening sensation by kneading the muscles of her lower limbs as though she were making dough, but the unseen parasites keep crawling.

Sleep is impossible. She rolls to the cold side of the bed but the emptiness makes her more agitated. She turns the bolster time and time again to relieve the torment, but it doesn't abate. She can hear the sound of her own sobs loud within her head and can find no way of releasing them.

To think that there was a time not so long ago that she'd lain here so incensed with rage that William was out drinking and squandering their future away that she'd fantasised about getting up and out of bed and running, crook in hand, to drag him home. In the end, what was the point? Now the anger has dissipated and changed into a feeling of being stranded alone on a far shore in the familiarity of her own bed. She knows exactly where he is now, but there is little comfort in any of it. Yet still the urge remains to rise and let her feet take her to where he'll be.

The night is dry and clear, the temperature low. She pads across the bare floor boards in the bedroom to the window, trying to avoid a tell-tale creak that might alert the family. They've been worrying. She sits on the low window seat and looks out across the village towards the estuary beyond.

She treads downstairs to the kitchen clutching the ramsons, throws on her coat and shoes and opens the kitchen door, closing it quietly behind her. No need for a lantern. The moon is waxing gibbous, wearing a halo of icy clouds around it like a diamond brooch, its surface almost touchable, drawn in sharp relief, shadow and light. Her thoughts take on the clarity of this night. Her feet will her to walk to where he lies.

The track to the church, silvered by moonlight, pulls her along. Dewdrops, perched on the tips of grass blades, are kissed by the light; the village green is transformed into an uncanny blue-tinted sea that she passes on her way to the graveyard.

At the church gate, she hesitates, seeing the inscription on the stone wall, but not daring to touch the scratched marks to the memory of the lost village of Llanelen. She thinks of her Ellen. Perhaps her fertility would not have been cursed, as it seems to be, had she not named her after this ill-fated village. What had good intentions and good heartedness done for those kindly village inhabitants who died or fled after being infected with typhoid? All they did was give succour to the survivors of a ship that went down in the estuary. She looks to that same estuary – still and silent now – full of secrets beneath its surface.

Opening the cast-iron latch handle, she steps into the other-world of the churchyard. Her way is marked out by primroses and wild daffodils as she approaches the porch. Tonight, she takes no notice of the lepers' stone tucked inside, but glides on, her grey hair loose on her shoulders. She passes ancient headstones near the porch, their stone covered in lichen, moves on past the older graves until she rounds the north tower, where the Thomas family grave lies.

Just as William had been called out of his bed by the first George, so now, William and George are calling her. To sit. To talk. She approaches the headstone. Generations of Thomases are buried here in the family plot: Sarah Jane and Josiah Thomas, William's grandparents; Hezekiah Thomas, William's father and George Idris Thomas, son of William and Eleanor Mount Pleasant. Her darling son, the first George.

The mound of earth is still raw from William's burial, though grass is gradually re-seeding now that spring is come. Eleanor traces her little George's name chiseled into the headstone. She's desperate to connect also with the letters that signify William's presence, but the stonemason has not etched the marks as yet. The soil needs time to settle. Apart from the humped earth there is nothing to prove that her husband is here at all. That he ever existed.

She sits on the grass at the side of the plot and talks out loud to William. Alone – but somehow not alone – she chunters on through the April night. She tells him how angry she is that he left her like that and in such a pickle. How she wishes she could have done more to help him. She tells him that George is now in the mines and Jack is making a good go of things at the farm. That things are going well with the wedding – but there'll be no drink. The boys have decided. Well, it's hardly surprising is it, seeing the way things turned out for him? He's a grandfather too, she says, a lovely, healthy little boy. They've called him William, after him. But of Ellen, she doesn't know what she intends to do. And who can blame her? After all, what's here for her now?

She doesn't realise that she is crying but when she takes her hand to her cheek, it is wet. She's tired too. A tiredness that she's never known before that seems to be wringing her out, like wet sheets going through the mangle. She wonders if she'll come out the other side clean and made anew.

She remains on the grass for a few moments to get her breath back, to try and mentally prepare herself for the trudge back up the hill to the farm. Just a few minutes more. There is such peace here. An almost perfect peace. But the reverie is broken by the screech of a barn owl in the branches of the yews, in the shadow of the hill.

She stands, turns in the direction of the noise and sees the almost white owl glide close to her, hovering, its wing beat silent. She swears that for a few seconds it holds her gaze with its amber-eyed stare. Then it is gone into the night, leaving only a single honey-tipped feather on the cobbled path. She stoops and picks it up, letting it rest in her palm. As she heads home, she feels lifted. She casts the ramsons aside to rot on the grass verge. She vows she'll hang onto to the feather. She decides that it is a sign of new beginnings and better times to come.

Chapter 28

A low front sweeps in off the Atlantic the week before the wedding. Gales from the south west lash the coast and bring salt-laden rain along the horizontal to Gower. Trees bend in submission, lambs huddle together and take shelter under blackthorn, and – in the exposed fields at the top of the village – earth-brown rivers run off the caked top-soil which is too dry to absorb the downpours. Tucked under the lee of the hill, Mount Pleasant escapes the brunt. It is relatively calm, both outside and in.

Jack sits at the kitchen table drinking tea, waiting for it to stop raining, the women chat about this and that; but mostly about the wedding.

"You nervous, Jack?" asks Ellen.

"Me? Nothing to be nervous about. Looking forward to getting it over and done with. Bloomin' fuss."

"No more Jack-the-Lad?"

"No. As I said. No more booze. Time to settle down."

"You're just a kid."

"Doesn't feel like. Lots to take care of with everything here," he says glancing around the room.

"You saying I'm a burden?" asks Eleanor.

"Course not. But you'll have to pull your weight, when I'm in charge here," he says, winking at Ellen.

"I won't make trouble," shouts Elizabeth from the settle.

"Take you out and shoot you if you do," says Jack.

"Aye, I'm about ready for the knackers' yard."

"Don't say that, Gran. There's plenty of life in you yet," says Ellen, realising that at ninety, Elizabeth can't have that many more years in her and that she'll likely never see her again when she goes back. If she goes back.

This morning, with the rain beating on the panes, snug around the fire with her mother in better spirits, Ellen feels she could, just, stay put. Not make any decisions at all but let life and fate decide what it would hand her. But then again, deciding to do nothing is, in a perverse way, making a decision without taking responsibility for it. It will all come out in the wash, as Elizabeth puts it. But is she, Ellen, a woman who can leave things to chance? She will meddle in everyone else's business, try to sort everything out, but when it comes to herself, what is she made of?

"Be nice to have Annie here," says Eleanor. "New blood."

Ellen knows what her mother means by that. Sometimes she can be so insensitive. Annie. Get her in. Get her settled. Get her breeding. Where does that leave her?

"Four women under one roof! Nice?" says Ellen, who feels like she's being squeezed out. Perhaps her decision is being made sooner than she expected.

"I'll miss George, mind," says Jack. Been joined at the hip for so long, sleeping end-to-end in that bed. Won't miss his chest, though."

186

"He's hardly going far," is Ellen's snide reply. "Isn't as if Malt Hall is Hoboken."

"No need to be sarcastic. What's got into you, all of a sudden?

"Nothing. It's just that sometimes everything around here is so small."

"Well, you'll be back where it's big soon, won't you? So no need to put us all down."

All the eyes in the room fix on Ellen's. But hers say nothing.

"Anyway, when Annie came around for the fitting, it got me thinking," says Ellen. "About what you could do to keep yourself out of trouble, Mother. Keep you busy."

"Busy? What d'you think I do all day?"

"I mean busy-busy. Money. New lease of life."

Ellen stands up and paces back and fore, her thoughts and words keeping time with her steps. The women – and Jack, fair dos – are an attentive audience as she speaks without taking breath, such is her enthusiasm for and belief in the scheme.

"You've always been good with your hands, Mother. They are *you*! Crochet. Knitting. Sewing. Annie said her mother remembers you were an excellent seamstress. Talk of the village. Though I told her you haven't been doing a lot lately. And that's a shame." Eleanor nods in agreement, face glowing with pride. "I thought, with Annie here, you and her could do something together, get some income of your own. It isn't as if you don't need the money. So, I'm seeing you doing sewing. Professionally. Tailoring, really: coats, jackets, dresses – and curtains and cushions. Right here in Mount Pleasant! And you could do the knitting and crocheting as well. The parlour is lying there idle. And there's more money in this than meat and veg and butter!" Eleanor shifts her bottom in the chair, sits up straighter to try and take in all that Ellen is proposing. "People could come to the house. Through the front door. The parlour could be turned into a workshop where you could measure-up, keep the fabrics. People could see you and Annie at work. What d'you reckon?"

"Well, you've been busy sorting my life out. And Annie's. Does she know about it?"

"Not exactly. But she knows I was thinking about something."

"Don't like to say it myself – and as you know, I don't like to brag – but you're right. I was very good at one time. Have a lot of skills that are going rusty."

"Better to drop than rust, Mother," says Jack, laughing. "Not like her in the corner."

"Not deaf, you know," shouts Elizabeth. And if you want the view of the aged among us, I think it's a fine idea, maid."

"Well, you can have a chat with Annie when she moves in. Be good. I can see it. What d'you think, Jack?"

"I just hope this front pushes through before the big day. Be a shame otherwise. Think it'll blow itself out by the weekend. Be in for a long, fine spell then."

Chapter 29

On the Thursday of Easter week, the bride and bridegroom, Annie and Jack, leave Mount Pleasant farm together as is the custom in Gower. Ellen walks close behind, and behind her trail Eleanor and George, who is drawing Elizabeth, perched in her finery, in a dilapidated three-wheeled bath-chair with a folded hood. She reminds Ellen of a toothless baby sitting bolt upright in a pram when she glances to see that Elizabeth is all right. It's hardly a carriage: William knocked it up out of odd bits of wood in his shed, and – like Elizabeth – it hasn't seen the light of day for years.

"Don't draw attention to me," she admonishes Ellen. "I'm not an invalid, you know. Don't want to detract from the happy couple."

Ellen smiles and turns back to watch Jack and Annie walk slowly down the track to the church. Jack was spot on. It's fine and dry and the sun is singling out Annie, the satin, lace and ribbon of the ivory dress reflecting in the light. Ellen was right. It isn't showy; it is perfectly Annie. The sun catches the red of her curled hair falling on her shoulders beneath the tulle veil, and it reminds Ellen of the lustrous coat of a fox at sunset. Quite magical.

Ellen wonders about the folk-lore, but she can't somehow believe in the aphrodisiac powers of the myrtle posy Annie is clutching. Its thick leathery leaves did indeed smell beautiful – strong, aromatic – when she rubbed the tips of her fingers along their verdant surface. But babies? Pragmatism always wins out over superstition in Ellen. Fertility can be predicted more reliably by the evident intimacy the couple already displays, the way they are leaning unconsciously into each other as though tugged by powerful magnetic fields. Or perhaps by the basic smell of each other, the way she was once attracted to Richard. Simple as that.

She can tell they already know each other *in a biblical sense* as her mother says, knows that the ladder was put up to Annie's window at night for Jack to climb up. Everybody knows about these things around here though they don't admit to it. Even though these things are said not to go on anymore, they do. The practice is still encouraged by some folk who feel the need to cling on to old ways of doing things, encouraging courting couples to test the waters. They are not supposed to go the whole hog, just a little bundling, kissing and heavy petting in the bed or on the straw, blanket between them, drawers left on. Matthias had encouraged it too when she was seeing Richard.

There she is again in the hayloft above the old cowshed in the yard at Prysg, tripping up the uneven stone steps to see Richard, who is already waiting for her. Lying entwined in a tight love-knot in the deep bed of dry straw, the tangy earthy smell of the threshed stalks married with his distinctive musky scent. Richard placing the blanket over the straw. Removing her bloomers firmly. Casting aside her chemise with a smile. Her lying on the makeshift mattress looking up at him as he stands unbuttoning his shirt and trousers, rolling down his long-johns without any embarrassment; just pride in his joy and gift for her. Sinking into the soft mattress with the weight of his body. The tautness of his muscles, the tightness of his buttocks. The taste of his breath. The salty sweat of his armpits. Gentle hands. Gentle voice. Hoarse whispers in her ear. The odour of his semen: soapy cleanliness mixed with the sea shore.

Matthias looking out of the kitchen window, willing it to happen like a puppeteer. He doesn't want her and Richard to just get close and intimate, above the waist stuff. He wants Richard to try her out, to go all the way, get her pregnant. Farm can't take the risk of a dud, a barren bitch. Has to produce tangible proof she can be bred, like the ewes and the heifers and the mares and the sows, like all the farm stock that keeps the farm profitable. The future depends on it.

She looks at Annie all fresh in her white dress and feels sullied, her thoughts at odds with the occasion. Yet why should they be? Why should she carry the burden of shame that she couldn't conceive as if it was an inherent fault? God, she loved him then. The rejection was more painful because of that: she was discarded like chaff to the wind. Who was she kidding? She'd have gone willingly to the kitchen at Prysg if things had worked out. She'd have put up with Matthias and tended to him and Harold in that unloved mausoleum of a male household if she was with Richard and a baby of her own blood was born.

But after the casting aside, she built a shell around her and fabricated the self-delusion that she didn't want to stay in Gower. Not at all. Her? A free spirit? Her feet couldn't wait to march her away from this place: that was the story she told herself and those around her. She was too big for this little peninsula with its little-minded people and its bigots and inbred families. She was going to where she could fly unencumbered and be modern; be more than a woman who simply did her duty and issued a new addition to the bloodline every two years, to be bred till long after the heir was produced, as though the Tuckers of Prysg farm were some royal dynasty. She would not turn into her mother.

Now, as she trails Jack and Annie, dressed in her green taffeta dress, Ellen doesn't know who she is. Drifting somewhere in the middle of the Atlantic Ocean between Hoboken and Llanrhidian. There's no doubt that she has achieved some of what she feigned to be two years ago in the rush following the rejection. But here, looking at Jack and Annie and thinking about Hannah and her baby, and about Richard – even remembering and craving the smell of him lying between her legs – she is not so sure about anything. Would it always be like this? Would something suddenly appear like a way-marker and point her in one direction or the other? Or would she always be tormented by her two selves, constantly tugging in opposition to each other, wrenching each other apart: the very opposite of the power that was pulling Annie and Jack together like the moon on the tide.

She smiles – not so cynically now – at the rent Annie insisted on making to her beautiful hand-sewn ivory wedding dress to bring her luck and fertility. Perhaps later, she'll even accept the pin that Annie has stitched into its fabric that she'll throw behind her in the hope that Ellen will catch it and be married soon. Or even the sprig of myrtle that Annie will take from her bouquet and offer her to plant in the garden to grow and flourish for her own bouquet. One day.

Chapter 30

The congregation is settled before Annie and Jack make their entrance, Ellen traipsing self-consciously behind. They were waiting in the porch so that Eleanor and George can wheel Elizabeth up and put her in position close to the chancel steps to get a ringside view. The Thomas family are few in the pews on the left; the Jenkins family swell the pews halfway down the nave on the right.

Ellen knows it's him as soon as she starts to walk – as gracefully as she can – down the aisle, keeping close to Annie's left, ready to take the posy. He's in the front pews, behind Annie's brother Tom. She sees that his thick, dark hair, always so difficult to keep tidy, has been slicked into shape with oil. Sees the nape of his strong neck, his wide shoulders filling his best suit. She wonders whether, when he turns to look at Annie – or her – he'll be able to see her very recent thoughts about him. Is she perhaps transparent? Could he feel her wanting to touch the hairs on the back of his neck, run her fingers through his hair? She's glad of Annie's sensible choice of dress for her, with its long sleeves and high neck, all the blushing areas on her chest that could expose her are concealed by green taffeta. But when he turns and smiles at her, the blood rushes to her cheeks.

As the Wagner bridal march concludes, she takes the myrtle from Annie and vows she'll focus on the organist perched on the bench seat in front of the pipes in the midst of the choir stalls. It'll take her mind off Richard. Martha has been the organist at St Illtyd's and St Rhidian's for as long as she can remember. And a very bad one at that. Ellen watches her leaning back on her seat, straining her neck to get a better view of the proceedings, her rimless glasses balanced on the end of her nose, her big bottom spilling over the timber. After all these years, the parson still having to turn to give her the nod about when to start the introduction to 'Love Divine All Loves Excelling' or the twenty-third psalm, and her speeding up as the singing continues, the congregation not able to keep up, and her finishing well ahead. It is a welcome relief.

The reverie ceases when Jack and Annie make their vows. Ellen realises the seriousness of it all, the public commitment for all to see and hear, to promise in front of the masses and a God she doesn't acknowledge, to be with one person, in sickness and in health, till death do them part. Her mother did it. Elizabeth before her. And now little Jack and Annie. Could she ever do it and mean it? Was she too selfish to be happy? To hand herself over to another person? And she's confused too; angry, even. What's this promising to obey that Annie has to say but Jack doesn't? And what's this tying of hands together by the parson and this placing of the ring on Annie's finger but not Jack's. A prize bull comes to mind with a ring in its nose, and Jack, threading his rope through the brass and leading it, against its will, perhaps, back to Mount Pleasant.

Outside the porch, the wedding guests are herded into a group by the photographer who set himself up on the path with his camera, and stands there impatiently with the draping cloth. Ellen's in the front row, with Annie, inches away from Richard in the row behind. She wonders what he's thinking; if, perhaps this scene of the newly wedded couple that is going to be captured by the lens and frozen in time, could have been them at one time. Wonders if he mourned for her the way she mourned for him. In all this happiness, she feels sad. To feel grief for a living person is somehow worse than mourning for the dead.

"Bath-chair to the front, at the end!" barks the photographer.

"I'm not a bath-chair, boy," shouts Elizabeth. "I might be old, but I'm not deaf or invisible."

"It's all right," says George, and he draws his grandmother's home-made chariot to Jack's side of the group.

Ellen fiddles with her hair, smooths down the taffeta of her dress, sucks her stomach in and holds her breath. The camera will capture every aspect of her as she is here, now, in this place, for all time.

It takes forever, this performance. She's putting her weight on one foot and then shifting to the other, while the photographer is telling everyone to be as still as they can, shouting "Cheese" and then ducking under his dark cloth.

"Last one!" he shouts, finally.

Ellen squeezes one last smile out and prays that it will be over soon. Why are things so antiquated here, still? In America, Mrs. Randall has her own little Box Brownie. Lots of people she knows have them. She doesn't, as yet. But she will.

As the wedding party relaxes and makes its way back to the gate, Ellen notices the diminutive figure of Esther standing still on the bank among the gravestones in the shadow of the wooded rise. There's the black hat, the long dark coat. Distant and solitary, she's making her usual silent appearance at a church event without obvious intrusion, unnoticed by most. Judging by Esther's position, she will appear among the others, in black and white, once the photographer has developed his film. Little by little, Esther will take shape in the negative, be made clear in the print that is pegged up to dry. She might be a tiny speck in the distance, but she'll be forever bound to Ellen in that frame. Despite the warmth in the late April morning, Ellen feels a sudden shudder and hurries to catch up with family and friends.

The wedding party finds the wooden gates to the churchyard tied with white ribbon. Outside, a group of village children laugh and holler, demanding payment from the newly weds and their party trapped inside. Standing resplendent in her fine green frock, they look a sorry sight to Ellen: the girls pasty faced and thin, the boys also looking as though they could do with a hearty dinner to put some meat on bones. One little girl has a leg bowed from the knee from rickets. It makes her angry and momentarily ashamed, that although they don't have much at Mount Pleasant, they're not in abject poverty anymore, with George in his digs at Malt Hall continuing to help out and Jack doing well on the haulage.

Jack reaches past his fob watch and chain into his waistcoat pocket and pulls out a florin which he offers as ransom to the leader of the group on the other side of the gate.

"Please let us out," he pleads in mock fear.

"You'll have to pay," says the child with the dirty face and the dirty knees. "At least a tanner!"

"I'll make it worth your while," laughs Jack, and hands the boy the silver coin.

The boy holds it in the palm of his hand, staring down at it.

"Thanks, Jack," he says. "I'll let you through."

He unties the bow and the happy couple and their guests pass through under a shower of grain and a rain of gun fire as the older teenage boys of the village point their shotguns to the heavens and sound off a few rounds to wish the couple luck.

*

Ellen hears the violin before she reaches the parish hall. Although she's not much of a dancer, she likes the excitement of the folk fiddle getting the feet tapping and the heart pounding. Wishes she could play it herself, but they've never been much for music at Mount Pleasant, their only artistic talents being George's poetry and her love of reading and her odd attempt at writing a poem when she is in her most contemplative or dark moments.

The doors and windows are flung open wide in welcome; the sounds of bow against string inviting everyone in to eat and be merry. Ellen wonders if that will be possible for the men, since alcohol is off the menu, but hopes that it will be. At least it should cut down the risk of a fight.

Fair dos, thinks Ellen. The bidder has been busy, done a good job, urging all the guests to come armed with food and money for Jack and Annie as they start out together as a couple. In turn, the guests wish the couple well and place their jars of preserves and pickles on the trestle table in front of the stage. On the plates, they place home-made bread and cakes and half-crowns along with the odd sovereign.

The Jenkins family hired the hall and decorated it, as well as hiring the fiddler from Llangennith. The men assembled the tables and arranged the chairs while the women draped the cloths over them and placed wild flowers in jars of water: the last of the primroses and the first of the bluebells. Mount Pleasant itself fattened, killed and provided the pig that takes pride of place, glazed, crisp and golden on its stake above a spit behind the top table.

Ellen is ravenous. Always been a good eater, her mother told her constantly. She tucks into the pork that Annie's father carved with aplomb. The meat is tender and flavoursome; it tastes of anything and everything that the pig has ever eaten from the slop and swill. The crackling snaps and leaps across the plate under her fork so she picks it up with her fingers and consumes it with relish. After she finishes, she takes each finger to her mouth and one by one, sucks off the juice, not taking heed of the loud slurping noises she's making. Her mother gives her one of those looks that says: *Where's your manners? Not in America now.* Ellen wipes the grease from her mouth with her napkin and licks her lips. The napkin has not removed the fat from her lips entirely. She has the sudden sensation of Richard kissing her full on the mouth, tasting the pork on her. She wishes she hadn't been so enthusiastic about eating it. The smell lingers. It travels from taste buds to memory. Once when she was a child at school, Winnie Grove from Freedown farm told her about someone who had been burned to death in a house fire and that the smell of the burnt flesh was like roast pork. She wishes she hadn't eaten it.

Delving into the trifle erases the unpleasantness in a scoop. It's one of her mother's, wobbling in a scalloped glass bowl, brimful with thick cream and custard and sponge soaked with blackcurrant jam from the pantry. She goes back for seconds. Funerals might make you tired; but weddings make you hungry. She scrapes her dish, licks the spoon clean and takes a quick look at her reflection in the tarnished silver. Since her image is slightly distorted in the curve of the metal, she can't tell if she's pretty or ugly, happy or sad. She doesn't even know her own self.

Later, the tables are cleared and the chairs arranged around the walls of the hall. If only she could let her stays out to accommodate her bloated stomach. She feels like the cows when their stomachs are distended by too much gorging on lush clover pasture. Had she four stomachs like them, then perhaps they might accommodate the food she has just gorged. She is hot. Her indigestion makes it hard to breathe. She looks at Jack, cwtched up to Annie in the corner, wonders if he's got his sharp little knife that he uses for the cattle in his suit pocket. She'd like him to come running over and make a little jab into her belly like he does to the left side of the cows when they're dangerously full of methane. Not too deep. Nothing dangerous. Just enough. Oh, for the joy of releasing all that offensive gas. Perhaps joining a jig later on will help shift this discomfort. Until then, she'll have to sit things out in silence and suffer.

The fiddler's in full flow, spirits high on nothing stronger than lemonade. Ellen watches his old face, wrinkled but intoxicated with the energy of music making. The body of his beloved fiddle is nestled under his chin, his bow sawing the strings, his foot tapping, his knee bending, his whole body in harmony with the fiddling and the diddling of the Gower reel that is his speciality.

Annie and Jack start the dancing, standing opposite each other, beaming. One by one, couples join them, forming two parallel rows and weaving in and out, down the inside, down the outside. She's never been much of a dancer: two left feet, Richard joked. He's not dancing either: she keeps checking his whereabouts, though he hasn't gone far. He's in a huddle of men at the front, laughing and talking, oblivious to her.

The hall is moist and warm with the sweat of bodies; loud with the thumping and scuffing of shoes on wooden floorboards. Everyone looks so happy. Even though she's in this throng of people she knows, she feels isolated. Uncomfortable and alone on a hard-backed chair placed at the very edge of festivity in her own parish hall.

Chapter 31

Minutes later, sitting with her back against the limestone slab that's tucked tight into the hollow under the hill at the top of the village, Ellen feels the tension leave her body after the discomfort of the wedding. The stone is worn by the years and warmed by the sun. Comforting. Reassuring. Full to bursting with childhood memories of how she wore her dresses through at the seat sliding down this rock. The sliding stone, they all called it back then. She smooths the pimpled surface with her palm, wishing for the past to seep back into her skin, realising that there is no trace of the heart and vows she and Richard had once committed to stone.

The sun is low, but not quite down, and the light half-cooked, the colour of liver. It's quite still here, away from the racket of the dancing, not a breath of air. With her eyes closed, she breathes slowly and deeply, trying to inhale the dream-like magic of this early evening in late April. It's almost perfect.

At first she thinks she conjured him up in her half-sleep. But when she opens her eyes he's standing in front of her, silhouetted against the rusty scales of the mackerel sky.

"Thought I'd find you here," he says.

"Needed some air," she says, straightening up, adjusting herself.

"Headache?" he says, seating himself beside her.

"No. Just wanted a bit of peace and quiet."

"I looked across and you'd gone. Was going to ask you for a dance."

"Very funny," she laughs.

"It wasn't your feet I fell in love with."

"Leave it, Richard. Don't. Not now."

"I did love you, you know. Still do. Probably always will," he says, his right hand clenching into a fist and beating it repeatedly against his ribs around the area of his heart.

"Have you been drinking?"

"No such luck. Smell my breath." He leans close and exhales loudly into her face. "It's just –" he goes on.

"Just that you didn't dare stand up to your father," she says, feeling her chest tighten under the taffeta.

"It wasn't as simple as that."

"Seemed like it. Choose me and Daddy would cut you out of the farm. Simple as black or white."

"You make it sound as if I had a choice, Nell. Tell me. What choice did I actually have? Logically?"

"You chose your inheritance over me. Barren stock. Not fit for breeding, me."

"Don't ever talk about yourself like that. I never wanted you to have those feelings."

"But I did. Not anymore, though. Neither you nor anyone else will ever make me feel like that about myself. You've no idea of the depths I went to."

"I'm so sorry, Nell. I really am. I can only imagine. But please try and see it from my point of view, too."

"Your point of view? Your palm is greased with silver. Money not love."

"I'm a bloody farmer, for Christ's sake. It's what I've been brought up to be. In my blood. Don't know anything else. Couldn't have said no to Father and looked after you."

"Don't need looking after. Can look after myself."

"I'm sure you can. In America. But what could I have done if I'd up and left with you? Tell me that."

"Anything. Everything. Engineering for example."

"Why engineering?"

"It doesn't matter. Just a whim."

"Be serious, Nell. Who would have looked after Harold? What would happen to him and the farm after father's days? Unfortunately, being a farmer's wife is a way of life not just a love match. The future depends on it. It's all for nothing, otherwise."

"So I was a bit like an insurance policy that didn't pay out, then?"

Richard doesn't answer but hangs his head and searches out a loose stone, starts scratching at the rock with the pointed end of it.

"I lost out too, you know. Duty and all that. I lost you. And myself."

"You didn't lose me, you discarded me. Deliberately. Cast me aside." Her voice is alien: low and thick with emotion. She can feel the tears welling up inside.

"If only things could have been different, Nell. I'd have made you pregnant the first time we were together."

"Well, things weren't different. And they're not different now, so like you say: we both lost something," she says looking him straight in the eye with the bare-faced lie that could choke her if she's not careful.

"Is there anyone else in America?"

"They're queuing up," she says. "Knocking down the doors with their white chargers. But honestly? No, no one else. Still just me and Emily Dix. And she'll be off soon. You?"

"What d'you think? You're not that easy to replace."

"I know," says Ellen, smiling, hoping deep-down that he at least is telling the truth. "But give it time."

"You look beautiful in green, you know. Especially in this light," he says.

"You're such a fibber, Richard Tucker," she replies and, in contrast to the message in her words, she leans into him and presses her mouth to his.

With this kiss, she knows she is falling into potential chaos. All her control and self-denial is lost and she's light and directionless as a feather that is being carried on the breeze to who knows where.

Despite everything, he tastes as she remembers him: sweet and clean and to her liking. Their lips still fit together perfectly but in her hunger to kiss, for a moment their front teeth clash. Soon they fall back into the peculiar easy motion and rhythm that they used to share as a couple when everything was so seemingly uncomplicated and familiar and she wore him like a second skin.

"Beats dancing," she says as she comes up for air.

"Aye, beats dancing. No left feet here," he laughs.

"Do I taste of roast pork?"

"Aye," he says, licking the rim of her lips with the tip of his tongue. "Very tasty indeed."

And he smacks his lips loudly. "And there's something else I can taste too."

"Trifle, probably. Overdid it a bit, if I'm honest."

"No. Not trifle. More metallic. Can't put my finger on it."

Ellen draws him into the shawl of her arms and returns to the task in hand to divert his thoughts.

How long they hold on to each other and kiss, Ellen doesn't know. She doesn't hear the agitation in the air during that strange period between dusk and dark when birds search out a place to settle unseen until dawn breaks again. Doesn't see the murmurations of whirling starlings perform their aerial ballet, drawing patterns against the late evening sky. Doesn't mark the second that the dying sun drops down and finally disappears out west over the ocean.

But now it is dark. The blades of grass are wet to the touch; the backs of her thighs itching with the clamminess of her underthings which have absorbed the dampness through the seat of her dress. She feels wet right through. Within, even. And she knows it's not solely down to her shenanigans with Richard.

"I'd better make a move," she says, standing awkwardly and pulling the back of the skirt of her dress away from her legs. "They'll have a search party out for me otherwise."

"I'll walk you home," says Richard, "as much as I'd like you to stay."

"No, I'd rather you didn't. Don't want to get tongues wagging."

"But will I see you again?"

"Perhaps. I've got to come to the farm soon anyway – need to talk to your father."

"About what?"

"None of your business," she says touching the tip of her nose with her finger and then kissing him one last time, gently on the cheek.

At the verge of the hollow, Richard takes the track that forks right back to Prysg while Ellen takes the track that forks left, back past the parish hall and home to Mount Pleasant. With each step, she feels the warm wetness trickle from between her legs. She remembers the once-a-month sweet meaty smell of Hannah's morning breath in the bedroom all that time ago and wonders if Richard will perhaps fathom the meaning of this taste in her mouth, wholly new to him.

Chapter 32

As a young child, Ellen used to think her mother's warning against casting *a clout till May is out* referred to the month of May. But now, as she walks towards Prysg, the curd-coloured blossom that's dressing the hawthorns tells her otherwise. For some ridiculous reason, she admonishes herself: she has inherited her mother's irrational fear of the flowering hawthorn. *Don't invite death into the house,* she hears her mother say, as she did when she used to gather these curiously scented blooms, half-sweet and half-putrefying, and offer them to her as a gift.

Folk-lore. Nonsense, she reassures herself as she quickens her pace over Welsh Moor. Too much talk in this place of crows and portends and myrtle and miracles. She pushes it all to the back of her mind. Much more important things about to happen, so get a grip on things, focus on the task in hand.

She clenches her jaw tight as she plans her approach. She'll make Matthias forego the so-called land deal, give her family back what is morally theirs. With righteousness on her side, she feels taller this morning, less squat and heavy-hipped as she pounds the uphill track, as if virtue is giving her impetus. She'll turn up uninvited at his door just as he did at Mount

Pleasant. Why the heck shouldn't she? She didn't realise until now that the quest for revenge could be so exhilarating, overflowing as she is with nervous energy and adrenaline. Probably be like a wet rag when it's all over and done with.

Her momentum is thwarted as she makes the left turn off the track down the rough lane to Prysg. The farm gate is closed. No one is in the yard beyond. But nudging and nuzzling at the timbers of the gate is a young foal, chestnut coat and white blaze, pawing at the ground. It is so newly birthed that that it can hardly stand on its bowed, windswept legs. It has a frightened look, the whites of its eyes enlarged and over-bright. And it is completely alone.

It doesn't budge as Ellen approaches but continues to make contact with the wooden bars in a desperate attempt to rub up against anything that might replace its mother. Ellen is at pains to take the gate off the latch and ease herself through to the other side without frightening the foal or letting it into the yard. She shouts for Matthias and Richard, but no one comes. The sight of this foal – so scared and defenceless – changes her mood in an instant, takes the wind right out of her puffed-up sails.

She hammers on the front door, but to no avail. She peers through the kitchen window, but there is no sign of life within. She can feel her heart beating fiercely in her chest like the wing-flap of a trapped bird. This poor motherless creature needs help.

She walks towards the sheds and still nothing. And then she hears the sound of Jim the sheepdog yapping and sees him and Richard coming down from the fields towards the orchard where the ewes and new lambs are grazing.

"I've been shouting! Where is everyone? There's a foal at the gate," she says.

"And good morning to you, too," he says smiling, not mirroring her state of agitation but walking calmly over to the gate, opening it, picking up the foal and cradling it in his arms.

"Didn't hear you shouting. On my own here this morning," he says.

"What you going to do with it?" she asks, not acknowledging Matthias' absence. "It's so weak and frightened."

"We'll get her inside now. Warm her up a bit."

"What? In the kitchen?"

"Aye. Put her in front of the range."

Ellen trails Richard – the foal tight to his chest and Jim wagging his tail behind them – back across the yard. Richard pushes open the unlocked kitchen door with his boot and Ellen steps over the threshold.

It's been a long while since she was here, and the memories flood back. It's still very much a man's house. Bare. Functional. Just the basics. Devoid of frill or comfort. The range is alight, and the room warmish, but there's nothing on the hob, no smell of anything simmering in a pot, nothing prepared ready for later. Above the range hang odds and sods of men's clothing airing on the dolly. These look as though they've hardly seen a bar of soap or scrubbing brush: singlets, long-johns, night shirts, toweling nappies for Harold. Ellen glances at the orphaned foal. Turns away at the intimacy of the scene.

The smell of woodsmoke is thick in the air, yet the open fireplace off the kitchen is unlit and unlaid, just the ashes lying unswept in the grate. She could never make her mark on this place. It's too set in its ways.

She watches as Richard places an old blanket on the flagstones near the warming oven and places the foal carefully on the blanket, rubbing its coat roughly to try and get some warmth into the body. The foal's weak legs seem no longer able to hold itself up.

"Need to find a foster for this filly," he says. "Sooner the better."

"Has it suckled yet? Can you tell?"

"Born in the night, I think. Could have had first milk, but I'm not sure."

"Can we feed her till you find a mare who'll have her?"

"Aye, I'll fetch the bottle and teat and get some milk from the goats. You stay here."

Ellen sits on the blanket with the foal while Richard goes in search of milk. She places her cheek on the filly's chest and listens to its beating heart, absorbs her growing warmth and the earthy smell of birth and earth. She wonders what happened to the absent mare. Then her thoughts shift to Matthias and Harold, as there's no sign of him either.

After Richard returns, she watches him pour the goat's milk into the glass bottle and attach the teat. He places the bottle to his cheek to feel the warmth and she half expects him to flick the milk onto the back of his hand to test the temperature as if he were about to feed a baby. How is it possible that he's of the same blood and bones as Matthias?

He kneels down beside her on the blanket and puts his curved index finger into the foal's mouth, searching out the gums.

"Think it's had first milk, this one. Sucking on my finger. Should take the bottle till I find that mare."

He tips the bottle and places the rubber in the foal's mouth. She gags at first and wrenches her head but he perseveres until she gets the hang of it and starts suckling. Ellen and Richard don't speak but listen to the ravenous slurp of the suck and the glug of the swallow. They smile at each other as the milk level goes down in the bottle until it's completely drained.

"There. That's better, girl," he says to the foal. Ellen watches his face: overflowing with gentleness, love and something akin to pride.

"You'll make a lovely father one day, you know," she says, stroking his forearm.

"And you'd have made a lovely mother, too," he says. "I'll make us a cup of tea."

Ellen leaves the foal to rest and sits at the table, flicking through a copy of *The Preston Farmer* which is open to a spread about sheep drenching and parasites. Matthias comes to mind. Richard stands at the range, waiting for the kettle to come to the boil. Steam is starting to rise from the spout.

"A watched pot, you know..." says Ellen, looking up.

"Sorry?" he says.

"Never boils? Oh, never mind," she says. "Anyway, where's Matthias? It's him I came to see."

"Gone to his sister Ethel's in Upper Killay for a couple of days. Went yesterday. Be back tomorrow. Harold's staying on with Ethel to give him a bit of a break here. It's really hard sometimes."

"It must be," says Ellen. And in all her anger she has a genuine, if momentary, pang of pity for Matthias and what life has dealt him. Explains the way he is, sometimes. No one is all bad, are they?

She watches Richard at the range, his strong back to her, engrossed in the tea-making. A feeling washes over her: sympathy, sadness, regret, love and desire. She rises from the chair and walks towards him. He stays facing the stove as she approaches and wraps her arms around his waist and presses her body into his, burrowing her face into his shirt. She breathes in the smell of him. He's like the foal, all warm and filled with the smell of livestock and hard work and grass. This is the moment she wishes to savour for all time: pure instinct devoid of all reason.

"I love you, Richard Tucker, you know," she whispers, her voice muffled by the fabric.

"I love you, too, Ellen Thomas. But it just can't be. And it's the saddest story I know."

She takes her hands from around his waist and reaches for his face to feel the wetness of his tears on his cheeks.

He takes her hands in his, still without looking at her, and kisses her fingers. She places them in his mouth, just as he'd placed his finger in the mouth of the foal. And then he turns towards her.

She can feel his hardness pressing into her now, so she takes his cheeks and kisses him fully and firmly on the lips. He tastes of salt and a little fear. He picks her up and wraps her legs around his waist and carries her swiftly to the table without once taking his eyes from hers. There seems so little time and so great an urgency, yet they want the feel of skin on skin. She unbuttons his shirt, the top of his long-johns. He mirrors the gesture, unbuttoning her blouse and lifting her chemise over her head. She feels her hair crackling with the static. She unbuttons his trousers and his flies too and then he reaches beneath her long skirt and pulls down her drawers. Nothing is said but Jim nips at the back of Richard's legs and at his heels, not knowing whether it is a rough game or a physical assault that is taking place across the kitchen table. Not until it is all over does he stop his high-pitched yowling.

She feels like sleeping then, tucked up with Richard on a blanket in front of the range like the foal. But she knows it cannot be. She leaves, closing the kitchen door behind her, the smell of Richard on her hands and the scent of woodsmoke in her dishevelled hair.

Chapter 33

Ellen feels encased in the kitchen at Mount Pleasant and hopes that its stone walls might soon breach to let air in, or her out. Annie's already wrapped in an apron – the uniform of Eleanor – as though she were serving some kind of apprenticeship with no written rules. Three generations of females all gasping for space under the low-beamed ceilings. She knows she's going to have to make a decision soon. There might be four generations competing here before long, judging by the self-satisfied expression Annie doesn't stop wearing. Night after night, into the early hours, Annie and Jack's cavorting and giggling keep Ellen awake in her lonely little bed. Sometimes she wants to hammer the wall to tell them to put a stop to it. Some of us need our sleep, she longs to shout. In the mornings she is pallid and feels queasy with the lack of sleep. She can't stop yawning. Air-hungry, Elizabeth says she is. But Annie's blooming appearance and happy demeanour is just irritating.

When Jack comes in for his breakfast, he's bursting with energy, and has an appetite for food like never before. She notices the looks he and Annie give each other; how he winks when he pushes his empty plate away. Ellen thought she'd be delighted by all of this, but now she's disgruntled; jealous, if she's honest. There's an emptiness in the pit of her belly and an acid taste in her mouth. How it is possible for them both to gorge on each other all night long and then gorge on so much food after so little sleep, she cannot fathom. As for herself, she can hardly stomach anything.

"Built up a bit of an appetite, Jack?" she says sarcastically, one morning towards the end of May.

"Aye," he says. "Starving I am, all the time. Don't know what's got into me."

He reaches for another crust of the loaf that Annie is slicing from her place at the side of the table, always on hand, knife at the horizontal, just as their mother always does it. Eleanor's place has moved, so that she is now silent at Annie's side, overseeing operations like a smug newly promoted Sergeant Major.

Later, once Jack has gone back out into the fields, and the dishes have been cleared, Annie and Eleanor move to the parlour to engage themselves in their new venture. Ellen and Elizabeth are left alone in the kitchen together.

"Feel like a spare part around here," says Ellen.

"Know the feeling, maid. Wait till you're my age. At least you've got a choice."

"Some choice."

"Too much choice, if you ask me."

"Well, I didn't ask you. And anyway, what d'you know?"

"I just know thee, maid. That's all. What's picking at you? Not the Matthias business, is it?"

"I went to see him to sort it out. But he was in Upper Killay. Having a break from Harold."

"Poor dab. But listen, you can't sort out everything in life, you know, just because you want to. Some things just sort themselves out."

"I need to do this for Mother. For the family. Tie everything up."

"Before you go back?"

"Yes, before I go back."

"For whose benefit, maid? Theirs or yours?"

"Theirs, of course. Why d'you ask?"

"Just let things be. And you shouldn't feel guilty, either. There's nothing for you here, is there? Not now."

"No. Nothing. Not now," says Ellen, her eyes filling with tears. "But I wanted Mother to have the Croft back. You know, for her pride. Her place in the village."

"I know."

"She's always talked about building a little stone cottage there sometime in the future. A place that perhaps George can come back to or perhaps Jack and Annie's child one day, or even George's if he ever gets his head out of his books. I just wanted to do my bit."

"Leave it lie, maid. Don't stir things up anymore."

"That's it, isn't it. 'Let things lie. Don't stir things up.' I'm not like that, Gran. I want to make things happen."

"You'll have a job and a half around here. Make yourself ill, you will."

"We'll have to beg to differ. Much as I love you, Gran, let's agree to disagree," she says, giving her a big hug.

"You're all skin and bones, maid. Flesh is falling off you," says Elizabeth as she embraces Ellen. What's the matter?"

"Nothing. Tired, that's all. Lack of sleep with the love birds."

"You look peaky. All in. Only seen that look on a face twice in my life: and I don't think you're dying. Too cantankerous to die young," says Elizabeth.

"I'm fine. Be better soon."

"I'd take it easy if I were you, maid."

"Like I said, Gran. You're not me, are you?"

Chapter 34

Ellen wakes to the room spinning and a nauseous feeling in her stomach. The aroma of bacon cooking in the kitchen wafts up the stairs and she leans over the edge of the bed and retches into the chamber pot. She inspects the contents, but it's just bile, which leaves a foul taste in her mouth and a burning sensation in her throat and nostrils.

Light is forcing its way in through the gap in the curtains and she turns her eyes away to avoid the glare. She won't get out of bed. Not yet. She'll put her head back down on the pillow, close her eyes, that should sort it out.

But it doesn't. Despite the nausea, she feels empty and has a longing for food, but the very thought of the bacon downstairs makes her heave again. A piece of toast would do it, no butter, no dripping. Or a dry biscuit. Something plain to settle the stomach.

She raises her head and swings her legs over the side of the bed in an attempt to get up but she is reeling still and an overwhelming tiredness is overcoming her. She wasn't as tired as this after her journey home from America, didn't feel as sick as this when the steamer bucked and swayed in the heavy Atlantic swells. For goodness' sake, pull yourself together, she says to herself. Just a migraine again. Or the brewing of some nasty bug that's knocking you off your feet.

She pads to the washbowl in the corner of the room, takes the jug and pours water into the china bowl. Supporting herself with her left hand against the wooden stand, she splashes her face with the cool water and wipes her lips with the flannel: the corners are caked with saliva. She lifts her head and takes a look at her reflection in the mirror. Elizabeth was right. She looks like death warmed up: drawn and pinched, white faced, dark circles beneath her eyes. She's never looked quite like this before, not even with a thunderous migraine.

She sits on the edge of the bed and tries to get herself together. As she does this she starts to think and something clicks. Then she starts to count. Every finger is a day since the Thursday of Easter week. She counts in sevens. Six sevens make forty-two. Though it's all relatively new to her, she's been having her periods every thirty-three days. Thirty-five days a couple of times. This makes it seven days late. But her breasts are heavy and sore as though she will bleed at any minute. But heavier and more sore. She strains her neck to look down inside her nightgown to examine them. They are firm. No, not firm; rock solid yet tender, blue veins radiating from the browning nipples. It can't be. This wouldn't happen so soon if it were. Surely not. Then she remembers Hannah telling her that she knew she was pregnant even before she was late with her period. She just knew, she said, by the change in her breasts and even the sudden thickening of her waist. Ellen prods and pokes her breasts, feeling for answers beneath the winceyette, presses her belly for tell-tale signs. But she really doesn't have to. She knows that something is indeed brewing inside her, deep in the dark mysterious recesses of her body. A something that could brew a storm outside as well as in. She is going to become a big-bellied woman after all, and the sudden sensation of power and satisfaction it brings, shocks her to her gut.

"Thought you'd died on us, up there. Was going to knock the ceiling with the broom to wake you," says Eleanor, as Ellen comes into the kitchen, fully dressed. "Come and have a cup of tea. Look like you've seen a ghost."

As she takes her seat at the table, Elizabeth catches her eye and gives her one of her looks. Ellen realises, in that brief glance, that she's been seen through. Yet she knows her secret's safe with her grandmother for as long as it needs to be.

Eleanor pours Ellen a cup of tea, yet even the mild perfume of the leaves in the strainer is too strong this morning. Ellen gags on the black liquid. Pushes the cup to the centre of the table.

"You sickening for something?" asks Eleanor. "Not like you to be off your tea."

"Headache coming on, that's all. You know how I get before it starts. Peculiar, it is."

"Nice piece of toast will do the trick. I'll get a slice on the fork now."

"That's just what I fancy. No butter, though. No crusts, either. Not this morning."

"And when you've had that, you need to go back to bed, girl, or you'll be fit for nothing. We can manage without you, can't we, Annie?" she shouts towards the pantry.

Ellen doesn't reply. Doesn't know whether she should feel relieved or irritated. Even though Annie is out of sight, her little frame is filling Mount Pleasant already. Ellen can feel the quiet might of it nudging her out of the door. Yet at that moment, she doesn't care, she feels so ill.

Ellen pecks at the bread like a little bird, struggling to keep it down. But she can play this game: what the eye doesn't see, the heart doesn't grieve after.

"Go on up, you. I'll fill you a warming pan and bring it up. Know it's June but it will give you a bit of comfort and get you to sleep. If you're no better, I'll get Jack to call for the doctor."

Why her mother is being so acquiescent, she doesn't know. It makes her feel redundant. Superfluous to needs. Yet, she is living proof that she is not redundant anymore, not superfluous to needs as she seemed to be at one time.

She takes her leave from the table; her gleeful smile is lost on her mother but not on Elizabeth.

"Try and have a good sleep, maid. Things are always clearer then," says Elizabeth, winking at Ellen as she escapes the confines of the kitchen for the sanctuary of her bedroom where she knows she won't waste her time sleeping. There's too much to think about. "And try not to be too clever for your own good." Her grandmother's voice follows her up the stairs.

Though the bedroom remains dim with the curtains drawn, things do indeed swiftly become clear to Ellen. Tucked up in bed with the warming pan wrapped in a sheet resting against the small of her back, she feels comfortable, almost like a little girl again. A little girl with a big plan.

She never thought of herself as deliberately manipulative before, though her father had once playfully referred to her as *a little schemer* when she tried to pull a fast one with a feigned headache in the hope of getting a day off school. But it hadn't worked. Bossy, yes; opinionated, maybe; controlling, definitely. But never before has she consciously felt the need to engineer a situation for her own end, never before felt such clout in being a woman, having such natural ammunition as bargaining power. There's a wickedness in it that she relishes. It might be her undoing in the end – whatever the end might be – but for the moment, she's going to run with it.

She's got her copy of *The Pilgrim's Progress* down from the bookshelf again, a sheet of blank paper against the hardback cover to press on, a blacklead in her hand. Committing her plan to paper will making it all seem real; doable. Jotting down the pluses and minuses will illuminate the risks and the personal gains and losses. All she'll have to do then is put the plan into action. What she can't guarantee is Matthias' reaction to it all. But she thinks she knows how to bait him, how to make him play into her hands. And of course, Richard's reaction, if and when he finds out, because at this stage he's not in the equation at all.

Chapter 35

It's oppressive weather for the second week of June, the sky the colour and weight of limestone. As she sets off alone from Mount Pleasant for Prysg, the midges are out in swarms – "thunder bugs", her mother calls them. Elizabeth calls them "no zee 'ems". Ellen acknowledges they're both right, as the almost invisible little blighters are nibbling at her neck and ankles more than usual, perhaps attracted by the new hormones that are coursing through her veins or perhaps a different scent that she is giving off. And yes, she won't be surprised if it does thunder. There's ozone in the air. She can smell it. No doubt the rain will come soon. She hopes so. Doesn't like a dry storm.

The nettles are hip-high along the track and alive with horse flies. Ellen wishes she had a tail to swish them away, as no doubt she'll be bitten alive as usual. They're homing in on her, around her head and wrists. The dark blouse she's chosen to wear and the speed of her walking doesn't help. By the time she leaves Prysg later, she'll be stung by more than just all these insects: she know that she may well be prey to Matthias' tongue, horrible bloodsucker that he is.

She turns into Prysg, opens the farm gate, remembering the

filly. Though there's no sign of the foal now, she caresses her own belly protectively as she walks across the yard. She's certain now that Richard is not there, since Jim is tied to baling twine attached to the rusty ring on the shed door. As she approaches, the collie runs around in circles, chasing his own tail, belly grazing the yard. She ruffles him behind the ears, and the dog stills and licks her hand.

"Good boy," she says. "Left you with the old bugger, today, has he? He'll be back later. Wish me luck."

The dog is quite calm by the time she walks over to the kitchen door and raps on it.

She hears the latch being lifted, the door creak open. Face to face, across the threshold, stands Matthias.

"Ellen?" he says, perplexed. "He's not in. It's Wednesday, girl. Livestock sale on at Reynoldston."

"Yes. I know. Haven't forgotten. It's not him I want to see, Matthias."

"If it's about the land, then you'd better come in."

"Indeed it is, Matthias. Thank you."

It looks as if nothing's been touched in the kitchen since her last visit: everything is as it was – the smell of the woodsmoke, the draped washing, the faint warmth of the range. Though this time, Harold is here as well as his father.

"Won't you sit down?" Matthias asks, pulling a chair out from the table where Harold is sitting.

The drab grey oilcloth tablecloth is littered with the debris of Harold's breakfast: uneaten crusts of bread, smears of jam, spills of milk.

"Good morning, Harold," she says. "How are you? Did you enjoy your holiday at Auntie Ethel's?"

Harold lifts his head and looks Ellen in the eye. He doesn't respond in words but continues with a high-pitched monotone sound as he taps the convex edge of a silver desert spoon over and over again on the back of his hand.

"Don't mind him. He's happy enough," says Matthias as he sweeps the crusts into his hand and discards them, wiping the tablecloth.

"Are you sure? Can we talk in private?"

"Deaf to the world, he is. Pretty calm at the moment."

Ellen glances at Harold and the spoon, which he uses as some kind of pacifier, a route from a troubled world to a calm one where only he goes.

"I'm going to come straight to the point, Matthias. And in the light of what's gone on in the past, you might find it quite difficult to believe. But things have changed. Considerably."

"I know things have changed since your father's death, Ellen. And I'm sorry about that. But the land... as I said, it's mine, fair and square."

"I'm not talking about that, Matthias. Well I am and I'm not. Hear me out a minute."

"You're going to sign it over, then?"

"Please, Matthias. Just listen. I know it will come as a bit of a shock. You might not even believe me. But things have indeed changed. I'm pregnant, Matthias. With Richard's child."

Matthias emits a strange snort, his expression is half smile, half scorn.

"Don't be ridiculous. It can't be," he sneers.

"I remember those words of yours, Matthias. Telling my father why I was no good for the farm, as if I was a piece of meat. But that was then, Matthias. This is now. As I said, things have changed."

"You're lying, girl. You're... You're –" he splutters, trying to pluck words out of the stale air with his right hand.

"Go on: say it. 'Barren'. Well, it seems I'm not, after all."

"Impossible. You haven't even seen Richard. He'd have told me if he'd seen you. He's my son, after all."

"He doesn't tell you everything, Matthias. He's a grown man now, for God's sake. Not Daddy's little boy."

"Good God alive. Well, this puts a new complexion on things," he says, the hint of a smile coming to his thin lips.

Harold's high pitched humming gets louder and more intense, the pace of the spoon-tapping faster. Ellen looks at Matthias' face, sees all of his life's problems fall away with the years. Suddenly he looks like a younger man.

"Richard must be thrilled," he says.

"He doesn't know. And he's not to know. That's why I'm here," she says.

"I don't understand," he says, "it means everything can go according to plan, now."

"Whose plan, Matthias? Not yours. Not Richard's. Mine, this time. Never again will I be the victim of anyone's plan."

"What d'you mean?"

"This is my child. Not yours or the farm's."

"But you must marry Richard. His future depends on it.

The farm's. His. For pity's sake, look at *him*," he says, pointing to Harold.

"Too late, now, Matthias. There was a time when all that would have been acceptable. Enough, even. But not now."

"But the shame. You can't stay here with a baby on your own. It's not done."

"I'm not staying here. I'm going back to America. And here's the plan. Unless you let my family retain the Croft, legally, with no further demands or knocking on doors, I'll tell the whole world that I'm pregnant and that your son has refused to marry me. It's you who'll have the shame this time, Matthias. And much as I don't want to hurt Richard, I have to put myself and my family first. You, for one, should know what that feels like."

Pleats return to Matthias' face: deep furrows along his brow – below his cheeks – as if it's just about to cave in. Ellen sees him grab hold of the chair-back to steady himself. She has an image of him standing there, dissolving into liquid and draining away between the cracks in the flagstones.

"Please don't go back, Ellen. We need you. All of us."

"I'm sorry, Matthias. I just can't. I'd die a slow and lingering death, from the head down, if I stayed here and came to all this. So please, I'm begging you. Don't tell Richard."

But she knows the little worm – Matthias – well enough to know he will.

Priding herself on the performance of her life, Ellen rises from the chair with feigned desperation darkening her face. The wind is up by now: that strange quick-rising offshore gusting heralding a coming electrical storm. It blows in through the window that has been left on the hasp, ruffling the thin curtains, and her hair. She notices Harold has put his hands to his ears, palms slapping them repetitively. She has no idea whether it's the tension in the room he's blocking out or that he has an inherent awareness – like a cat or dog – of the din of the thunder before it happens. She turns to go, leaving Matthias gripping the back of the chair, his knuckles as white and as tight as his face.

As she steps across the yard, rain starts to pour on the vertical, spots the size of half-crowns splatting the ground. A flash of sheet lightning follows. She counts the seconds until the first rumble of thunder as she draws the iron bolt tight across the farm gate and heads for home. She lets the rain douse her uncovered head, enjoys the cooling deluge on her face, though it does nothing to temper the irritation of the red-raw weals that are appearing on her wrists, nor to drown out the memory of Harold's high frequency thrum. Above it all, her father's voice: *you little schemer, you.* Though this time, there is no lightness or humour in his tone.

Chapter 36

The days are long but the time is short. This is one of Elizabeth's favourite adages, which she throws out from the pulpit of her settle from time to time. Ellen knows that for Elizabeth, the idiom is coloured by her own experience of waiting for death. But by the third week of June, the words have taken on a specific meaning for Ellen, too.

The daylight hours increase as the solstice approaches. At each chime of the hour and each dawdling tick of the clock, Ellen wonders if the longer days will give Matthias more opportunity to come calling. He may well charge – like an incensed bull – into Mount Pleasant, to call off the contract with which she thinks she has verbally bound him. Or worse. She wonders whether Matthias might have confided in Richard and he'll come – like a knight in once-shining armour – offering his hand in marriage, a future on the farm. She can't bear the thought of having to choose between life back in the US or one here in Gower if – it comes to that. It will come soon. The dilemma. And the time she has left at Mount Pleasant is not long.

The tickets from Liverpool to Ellis Island have been finalised, the Gladstone bag packed once more, ready for the return journey. She has tucked *The Pilgrim's Progress* – stuffed with old, sentimental love poems and more recent lists – deep into the recess of her bookshelf in the bedroom. She doubts she'll ever see the book again. Wonders if those who take her room after she is gone – perhaps those not yet even born – will ever take down the book, delve into her mind, try to fathom out what she is made of.

The family is all assembled down below. Whenever something important is happening, it's always food that brings them together. Funerals. Weddings. Homecomings. Leave-takings. Ellen can hear the hunger cry of Hannah's little William reach a crescendo and then suddenly quieten. Must be taking the breast. She suddenly feels her own breasts tingle, and she rubs the swelling flesh in sympathy and to reassure herself that this is actually happening to her. No one apart from Elizabeth has an inkling. This is the final show she'll have to put on.

"What's this, then? The last supper?" she asks as she breezes into the kitchen.

"No need for that, Ellen," says Eleanor. "Have a bit of decorum. Trying to do something special here to give you a good send-off. Always having to hide how you're really feeling by being flippant, you."

"Forgive me, Mother, for I have sinned," says Ellen, looking around the room for laughs.

"See?" says Eleanor. "No one is amused. And that's blasphemous. So don't!"

"D'you think I'll be struck down, then?" asks Ellen.

"Don't push your luck, maid," pipes up Elizabeth from the corner, with a knowing wink. She's manouevering herself out of the settle, accompanied by a great deal of sighing and getting to grips with her walking stick.

"We've gone to a lot of effort for this," says Jack.

He's standing at the head of the table, in front of the carver, as though he's been standing there all his life.

"Nice leg of lamb. Killed and butchered it specially for you, sis," he says as he slices the meat off the bone and onto the plate.

Ellen sees him morph into their father. All the fathers, the grandfathers and the long line of male Thomases that have ever sat in that chair, that will sit in that chair in years to come.

"Ah, the sacrificial lamb," she says. "I'm honoured."

"That's what we're trying to do," says George from his chair at the side of the table. "Don't spoil the moment."

Ellen gulps. Yes, this is a slice in her life. Once upon a time. Never to be relived. She must savour it. Drink it in, for once it is gone it is gone and can never be repeated. Her memory will carry all the loss of it. Elizabeth creaking to the table; Hannah feeding William under a woollen shawl; Hannah's husband Charlie, quiet as usual; Jack with his sharpening steel in hand; Annie, so close to Jack that she could be sewn into the seams of his trousers; George, getting more serious and more tight-chested by the minute, and Eleanor, like a trusty shire horse, wearing the tiles out as she plods back and fore on her never-ending mission between stove and table.

"Not going to change your mind then, Ellen?" asks Annie.

One of little William's tiny hands is clutching at the wool of Hannah's nursing shawl. Ellen can hear him glugging as his mother manages to eat – with just a fork – the food that was cut up earlier by Charlie into bite-sized chunks, as though Annie herself were a baby. She wonders if anyone will ever cut up food for her, place a muslin square on her shoulder. She notices, though, that when it comes to changing the nappies, Charlie makes himself scarce.

"No, my mind's made up. It's for the best," Ellen replies, unsure at that moment whether it is or not. "After all, nothing to keep me here now."

Elizabeth clears her throat. A bit too loudly for Ellen's liking. She casts a long dark look at her. "You've done all you could, maid," she says with an honesty that Ellen finds satisfying. "You couldn't have done anything to save your father. None of us could. Don't think he wanted to be saved."

Hard to think it's been six months since she received the letter begging her to come home and work her magic with her father. But no, not even she could save him. She who still thinks she can pull the strings and the whole world will dance to her wishes.

"Think you're right, Gran. You usually are," she says. "Seems like nothing has changed, yet everything has."

"Let's not get all maudlin, now," says Jack. "Things are on the up. Mother and Annie are set to take the world by storm from the parlour – and that's down to you, Nell. And young Longfellow here – he's got things worked out at the mine and has a captive audience into the bargain. The haulage is coming along. So you're leaving us in a better position than we were when you came. So thanks for that, sis."

"Really?" she says.

"If it wasn't for the Croft, we'd be laughing," says Eleanor. "Matthias won't let us off that. I know him," says Eleanor.

"I think he will, Mother. Trust me. He's come to his senses."

"What makes you think that?"

"Female intuition," she says, pointing to the tip of her nose. "He won't be bothering you again about that. Not now."

"It isn't that I don't trust you. And I won't ask what you've been up to, but I'll believe it when I see it."

"Don't you believe in miracles, Mother?"

"No. Not anymore. You?"

"D'you know, I just think, I might? What about you, Hannah?"

"Well, things are better at the pub. Trade more steady, isn't it, Charlie?"

"Picked up a bit over the last few weeks. Not knocking the doors down, but dribs and drabs."

"Said it wouldn't last, didn't I? Blown himself out, he has like a south westerly gale. Impossible to keep that going."

"Not so many turning up to hear him preach, they say. Back on the beer," says Hannah.

"Well, I never thought I'd be pleased about that," says Eleanor.

"Just a fad, he was. Fraud, if you ask me," says Ellen.

"No one's asking you, Ellen, but that never stopped you

spouting your opinion, has it?" says George, joining the conversation.

"Back swearing underground, are they? Beating their wives again?"

"No, they're not, actually. They're still liking a bit of the Bible along with me reciting poetry."

"Good to hear. Long may it last," says Ellen, not convinced.

"Don't start. Not today of all days," says Eleanor. "You might never see your sister and brothers again."

The finality of the statement stuns the table into silence. There is just the sound of cutlery against china, Elizabeth's chomping on toothless gums, the slurp of tea, little William gurgling away, full and content under the shawl. It seems like years to Ellen, and she longs for something to relieve the tension and bring home the reality that tomorrow she'll be on her way. Yes, the days are long; but the time is short. And then a long and liquid explosion erupts beneath the shawl and everyone around the table doubles up with laughter and mock embarrassment until their sides ache and tears run down their cheeks.

Chapter 37

This is just as she'll choose to remember Mount Pleasant. Mid June. Cloudless sky. The merest hint of a breeze that carries the scent of summer flowers. In full bloom, they grace the front garden, heads turned to face the morning sun: stocks, lupins, hollyhocks. For a few moments as she stands there breathing it all in to store it up, even the marigolds look beautiful.

That's it, though. Things are not as they seem, are they, most of the time? You can only choose to believe a particular truth at any given moment. The truth of this place is that it rains for over two hundred days a year, that the wind blows incessantly from the south west. Ellen looks at the trees in the lane as if to prove a point to herself. And at the marigolds. There's always another side to everything. Another truth. According to her mother, it was spending too long growing marigolds and gazing at their burnished petals that turned her father to drink. Though she never admitted that it was an illness. More like: being weak; succumbing to the devil. Ridiculous.

The truth of this place is that it's stuck in time. And as beautiful as it is, and as much as she loves her family and

Richard, unless she wills her feet to walk away, she'll be rooted to this troubled paradise. Fixed in a kitchen at Prysg with two grown men, a child-man and a child yet to come. *The trouble with you, my girl, is that you just can't be content. Nothing's ever enough. You'll never settle,* her mother has told her often enough.

Why should she settle? What does it even mean? Is settled something like her mother? Deep inside, was she really settled? No, if that is what being settled means, she'll leave it to the cream in the dairy. She'll never have her Box Brownie if she stays here. But standing in the garden, she is unsettled, her stomach resembling the contents of the milk churn.

It would be so easy to change the course of her life, by opening her normally big mouth and letting the words spill out. She would tie up a lot of loose ends by doing that. Make people happy. But what about Ellen herself?

One second the sun is shining, just as it is now. There she is with the baby at her breast, Richard at her side, the kitchen at Prysg sparkling clean, the table set for supper. Harold calm at the table with his spoon. Matthias whistling. And then it's raining again, she's at the range. Harold's old now, hunched over the table, head in hands, emitting a long, painful whine. Matthias is dead and it's just her and Richard on the farm and the eldest boy, waiting his turn. She sees the expressions on the faces of Richard and herself, how their mouths turn down at the corners, how the lust and the longing has vanished from their eyes, how the days are long, but the time is short.

How will she ever know if she's doing the right thing and how things will turn out in the end? But there is no end, only death. Life is so untidy. All those ends that keep fraying, unravelling. She could toss a tanner and leave it to fate like her father. Or she can go with her gut. With that below-the-eyebrow feeling that's connected to her feet and is urging her to walk away without looking back.

Celt's standing at the ready in the yard, tethered to the rusty old ring on the stable. The boys have worked together to get him spruced up, as they used to: Jack's polished the brasses and George, the leathers.

"He knows something's up. Can sense it," says George.

"Don't say that. Makes me upset," says Ellen.

"I'll put your bag in the back," says Jack. "Time to get moving."

This time it's her grandmother, mother and Annie who are standing in the yard, ready to wave her off. In turn, youngest to oldest, she kisses and squeezes them goodbye. She takes in their distinctive smell: Annie's fresh and young, still new to Ellen; her mother's, so familiar, she can summon it at will whenever she chooses to remember; and Elizabeth's, that singular odour that old people get: a mix of camphor, stale breath, oily hair. All of them she inhales as though to get her fill and carry with her.

"We're going to miss you, you know. More than you'll believe," says her mother, dabbing her eyes.

Ellen wonders if this is true. Whether Annie, too, is breathing a sigh of relief that she'll be able to find her feet with Ellen's gone.

"You look after yourself, maid, d'you hear? Want to know how things turn out in Hoboken, so make sure you write to your dear old Gran."

"I will. Promise."

"There'll always be a home for you here," says Eleanor.

"Yes. Make sure you keep my room as a shrine," jokes Ellen behind the tears.

And then she's up into the front of the cart, wedged between George on one side and Jack, at the reins, on the other. As Celt walks on slowly from the yard, she turns and waves one last time, to the figures fading away as she rounds the bend. Even though the women have disappeared from view, she's still looking back. There in the distance, in the lee of the hill, a familiar figure catches her eye: the black hat, the long shapeless dark coat, the heavy flat boots. The sight makes her swallow. Her leave-taking is an event that Esther feels obliged to witness. Ellen waves in acknowledgement but the gesture is not returned. Esther remains, standing stock still in the shadow of the hill, and slowly becomes nothing more than a speck.

"What's she turned out for?" Ellen asks her brothers, and shivers. "C'mon. Let's get a move on."

Jack instructs Celt to gee up as they approach the rise out of the village.

"You sure?" asks George. "You don't have to, you know."

"But I do, George. No turning back now," she says.

At the crossroads, she turns her head right to snatch a final glance at the winding track towards Welsh Moor, and Prysg beyond, out of sight. Half a mile, yet already an ocean apart. She straightens up, faces forward, weaves her arms into her brothers' and listens to the echo of Celt's shoes on the track towards Gowerton.

"You nervous about going back?" asks Jack.

"Be all right once I get there. It's been my home for two years, remember. And Mrs. Randall is like a mother to me. Perhaps more of a mother than Mother, if you know what I mean. No sparks."

"Well, tell her to look after you," Jack said.

"I'm sure she will," says Ellen, crossing her fingers. "Let's hope so, anyway. I feel in my water that she will."

With Celt at a trot, there's a welcome breeze in her face now as they approach Penclawdd. The nausea is still affecting her. She unlinks her arms from the twins' and rests them on her belly. She knows she is still safe in the time that's left: the boys have no idea. Yet she can feel the gentle swell of her abdomen beneath the folds of her skirt. The waistband is cutting into her girth. She's discarded her stays. The thought of them is enough to give her a feeling of tightness. Once she's on that train she can breathe out. Be the big-bellied woman she never thought she'd be, in complete anonymity for a week or so. For who knows how much longer. Until she starts to show. Until Mrs. Randall starts to notice. She doesn't know how it will play out then but she's hoping there will be a room there for her. She has a feeling that Mrs. Randall would welcome a new life in the house. It's just a feeling, though.

As they round the bend into Penclawdd, it seems to be a

reversed mirror of her journey towards home six months before: topsy-turvy and back to front. The station master is closing the gates, the marsh ponies are still standing fetlock deep on mounds of grass above the tide on the ebb; the stench of brine and shellfish reeks remains. Ellen puts her hand to her mouth to stifle a yawn. Continuous wide-mouthed yawning is always a tell-tale sign that she's going to be sick. She brings her clean cotton handkerchief to her mouth and retches slightly behind its cover, sweating slightly but safe in the knowledge that the boys haven't noticed.

"Not long now, sis. Nearly there. Have you on the train in no time," says George.

"Aye. Best to get going when you've got to go," says Jack.

"I hate goodbyes," says Ellen. "Need to get it over and done with now."

Her mind fills with images of the last few months, all out of sequence, stuttering frame by frame in sepia tones to the accompaniment of Celt's rhythmic trot. She tries to filter the grotesque from the beautiful, life from death or near-death. But it isn't simple. As she's so fond of reminding everyone else, life's not black and white. And she's firmly in the grey area now. She closes her eyes. Tries to shut him out. Yet, Richard's face is floating in, time and time again.

She knows it is love, or what love means to her. Flawed and imperfect though both love and she herself both are, she knows that with him she feels as close to her real, good self as she thinks possible. It is perfectly easy and without pretence. She knows that it is the same for him, too. If they could exist in isolation, both shake off the constraints of Matthias, the farm, even society in Gower, in Wales, even, then they'd thrive, or at least have a chance. She imagines them both on a little rented farm in Gower, where they could be free and he still work for Matthias as well, and she wouldn't have to endure life at Prysg, interned in that kitchen. There's a little white-washed cottage with woodland she's seen on the road to Llanmadoc. She's always loved it. Bracken Bower, it's called. The name entices. It's not far from Prysg at all, yet far enough. A romantic notion that she shuts out of her mind.

For a moment, she imagines him in Hoboken with her, beginning a new life, taking a risk. But he'd never leave the farm, would he? Never be free of his sense of duty, as she decided to be. With Richard in Hoboken – or maybe Rutherford – perhaps Matthias would have to turn to her family for help. After all, they'd be sort of joined, then, wouldn't they? She likes the thought of that, of moving the pieces in her jigsaw until everything falls neatly into place. Matthias would need some muscle on the farm: he'd be desperate to keep it going. For a few moments she conjures up George, removes him from the debris and the dark and damp tunnels out under the Loughor estuary and puts him in the light again, in the fields and meadows around Prysg. The fresh air will suit him. Breathe new life into him.

All mere fancy. She thinks back to the night of the wedding, the conversation with Richard at sunset under the hill at the side of the Parish Hall. He didn't question her further when she mentioned Emily Dix or the engineering.

Wasn't even curious, damn him. Why couldn't he imagine it all and let it seduce him?

Things are turning to dust. Not everyone marries the person they love; she's pragmatic enough to acknowledge that. She'll be happy. Happy enough. And he'll be on the farm carrying the weight of his inheritance rather than imprisoned by love. That's his choice. Though it's hardly a choice at all.

She can smell the smoke from Gowerton North before they pull up to a halt to tether Celt in the yard. It hangs like a pall over the roof of the station. Already the taste is on her tongue, irritating her nostrils. Her handkerchief will be black again in no time.

George takes down her Gladstone bag from the cart and offers to carry it for her. As always, she refuses. Together the three of them walk from the yard into the little station. Ellen looks up at the station clock. Fifteen minutes to spare. The train to Liverpool departs at the top of the hour, at ten o'clock. It's already there beyond the ticket master who clips her ticket before she steps onto the platform.

The hiss of steam as the boiler is being fired up is loud in her ears: thick, white vapour clouds the platform, partially obscuring the engine and the carriages. With her brothers flanking her either side, she manoeuvres herself and her heavy load through the gathering throng towards her allocated compartment.

And there, at the side of the locomotive – his dark hair slicked into shape, dressed in the best suit he wore at the wedding, a new leather suitcase in hand – him.

Acknowledgements

With thanks to all those who have inspired and supported me on *Advent*'s journey to publication: the Creative Writing department at Swansea University where its seeds were sown under the supervision of Stevie Davies; Rebecca F. John, friend and mentor, for her insightful questions and advice through the novel's early drafts; Gaia Banks, my wonderful agent at Sheil Land Associates Ltd. for believing both in me in real life, and in fiction, my central character, Ellen; all my fellow writers at Hay Writers At Work; my Twitter support team – Eloise Williams, David Lloyd, Cath Barton, Wendy White, Janice Leagra, Fiona J. Mackintosh, Michele Smart; my dear and very talented BAFTA-winning friend, Euros Lyn, for his close reading and outstanding film director's eye; as ever, my husband Philip, for his patience and encouragement: and finally, Caroline Oakley, Editor, and the Honno imprint, for giving the best home possible to my debut novel, truly made, rather than merely set, in Wales.

p. 95 Part of a traditional song that accompanied the Mari Lwyd – it varied in different parts of Gower. This verse was taken from 'Gower Gleanings' by H. M. Tucker published by The Gower Society in 1951

ABOUT HONNO

Honno Welsh Women's Press was set up in 1986 by a group of women who felt strongly that women in Wales needed wider opportunities to see their writing in print and to become involved in the publishing process. Our aim is to develop the writing talents of women in Wales, give them new and exciting opportunities to see their work published and often to give them their first 'break' as a writer. Honno is registered as a community co-operative. Any profit that Honno makes is invested in the publishing programme. Women from Wales and around the world have expressed their support for Honno. Each supporter has a vote at the Annual General Meeting. For more information and to buy our publications, please write to Honno at the address below, or visit our website: www.honno.co.uk

Honno, D41 Hugh Owen Building, Penglais Campus, Aberystwyth University, Aberystwyth, SY23 3DY

Honno Friends
We are very grateful for the support of all our Honno Friends.
For more information on how you can become a Honno Friend, see:
https://www.honno.co.uk/about/support-honno/